ALSO BY EMILIE GLEN

The Writings of Emilie Glen 1: Poems from Chapbooks

The Writings of Emilie Glen 2: Fiction and Prose Poems

The Writings of Emilie Glen 3: Poems from Magazines

The Writings of Emilie Glen 4: Poems from Manuscripts

THE WRITINGS OF EMILIE GLEN

2

FICTION AND PROSE POEMS

Selected and edited by Brett Rutherford

THE POET'S PRESS
Pittsburgh, PA

TABLE OF CONTENTS

ABOUT EMILIE GLEN

FOR MORE THAN twenty years, I was Emilie Glen's friend, fellow poet, and publisher. We met in the muggy summer of 1969 when I first arrived in New York City. From the mid-1960s until almost 1990, she was den mother and confidant to several generations of aspiring poets. She hosted poets twice a week — Sunday nights at her 77 Columbia Street apartment, and another night at various West Village lofts or theaters. In addition, we would meet at various old-fashioned restaurants: Schrafft's, Macy's Fountain, Rumpelmayers.

Although she rode to her dinner engagements on a bicycle, dressed in short skirts and pink leotards, red hair flying, Emilie was not the rag-tag Village Bohemian she appeared to be. She had been a child of privilege. Taken on the Grand Tour of Europe as a young girl, she had seen Paris, the Harz Mountains, Rome. Later, her family summered at Chautauqua. She trained as a child prodigy under concert pianist Ernest Hutchison, and continued on to Juilliard School in Manhattan under his tutelage.

Unlike the rest of us, Emilie did not have to go to work on Monday. Or Tuesday. She was provided for, modestly but securely. She was able to do what we all dreamt of: to devote her life to writing.

Emilie was married, but her husband, Charlie Dash, was absent and seldom mentioned. It was clear from Emilie's carefree ways, and her stunning indifference to financial matters, that her late father, and her indulgent husband, had left her financially independent, at least enough so to continue living in Manhattan to pursue her art full-time.

Emilie's apartment at 77 Columbia Street was in a respectable high-rise co-op, overlooking the East River. The Lower East Side neighborhood, bordering Delancey Street and the Manhattan Bridge, was quite sinister at night. Yet poets came each Sunday evening, year-round, by cab, car, or subway, in everything from jeans to fur coats.

When Emilie's folk-singing daughter Glenda married and gave birth to a child, the sudden death of the son-in-law (both alcoholic and epileptic), induced Emilie to make a drastic change in her living conditions: in 1979, she gave up the Columbia Street co-op, and sold her piano, to move into the brownstone tenement building at 77 Barrow Street to help her daughter care for her infant son, John. Emilie took the apartment adjacent to Glenda's. It was dark, narrow, only two rooms. The toilet was in the hall. Emilie slept on a narrow bed next to the kitchen, and turned the living room into the best semblance she could of her old parlor. The Sunday night readings resumed. The terrifying night walk down Delancey Street was replaced by the welcoming streets of Cherry Lane and Barrow Street. Walking up five flights of stairs was a small price to pay for the poetic thrills that awaited one. The Village location also meant that poets could repair to a local coffeehouse after the reading was over, for more poetry talk and gossip. Such nights often went on until the cafes closed (the Bohemia we have now lost forever in the Yuppie-infested decades since).

In giving up her piano, Emilie had made the final break with her first Muse. She had trained as a concert pianist, and so long as there was a piano in the house, she was never really severed from that early promise. Now she would only play, with faltering memory, when she came upon a piano in a café or in someone's home. The piano would now become a ghost, its notes sounding but never dying in her later poems. I never heard Emilie complain about the appalling condition of her apartment, with its bathtub in the kitchen and decrepit stove and refrigerator: only the loss of the piano seemed to diminish her spirit.

EMILIE Carolyn Glen was older — by decades — than she wanted us to believe. When interviewed, she would terminate the conversation when the delicate question of age came up. In the 1977 *International Who's Who in Poetry*, Emilie listed her birth date as 1927. In a later directory, she revised that to read 1937[1]. Actually, Emilie was born around 1906, making her 63 years old when I first met her in 1969. Her birthday was March 13.

Early in her career, she worked for Macmillan Publishing Company and did a stint with Fairchild Publications — from what I can gather, as a reporter for *Women's Wear Daily*. In a poet

---

[1] Emilie was listed in *Who's Who in U.S. Writers, Editors and Poets*, 2nd edition 1988, and in successive editions through 1995-96. Her birth date there was listed as 1937! She was also listed in *Who's Who of American Women*, 2nd edition, 1961-62 and 1964-65. I would be grateful to receive photocopies or transcripts of these listings.

biographical note in 1947, she indicates that she "covered fashion shows, visited wholesale houses, and saw child models at work.[2]" In this note, she says that her daughter Glenda was then seven years old.

Her university experience included a full course at Syracuse University. The sorority Alpha Phi Alpha lists her in the graduating class of 1928. Emilie continued to Columbia University and went on with her music studies with Ernest Hutchison at the Juilliard School.

At some point, literature took precedence over music. Emilie was not clear in her own mind why her career as a pianist ended, but the competitiveness and misogyny of the classical music field may have contributed. There were then only a handful of women among the premiere artists of the keyboard, and virtually no women in orchestras. In the literary world women, while embattled, could at least expect a modicum of success.

I suspect Emilie also realized that the choice between being a creative artist and a performing artist was one that had to be made. Many people could play Beethoven and Liszt; only Emilie could write Emilie's poems.

During the 1940s, Emilie worked on the staff of *The New Yorker*. Only a single, brief notice, in 1942[3], credits her as a writer there, however. She may have worked for the publisher as a behind-the-scenes fact-checker. Emilie related to me how *The New Yorker* checked every reference in every piece they published, even in poems. She recalled that a number of women hired by the magazine in the 1940s were let go at war's end when "the men came home."

Editing a Manhattan-based Congregational Church magazine appears to be Emilie's last paying job. Several sample copies were among her surviving papers.

She was an avid bird-watcher, and for many years haunted Central Park with binoculars, a member of that elite society of The Rambles. One story in this volume sprung from her observations of birds, and those who watch them.

Although Emilie had not traveled abroad since childhood, she, like Thoreau, traveled much where she lived. Her bicycle was spotted in all boroughs, and she would even venture by subway and

---

[2] *Epoch*, Cornell University, 1947.

[3] Russell Maloney, "Comment", *The New Yorker*, October 24, 1942, p. 11

bicycle to Far Rockaway. She was a year-round swimmer, and swam with the Polar Bears Club. Her stamina was incredible, as was her resistance to doctors and medicine. Some poems in Volume 3 suggest that she might have visited the Caribbean in the 1950s or early 1960s, an uncharacteristic vacation, but then, the sea was always Emilie's first love. The short story, "Waldron Hold," in this volume was almost certainly researched in Bermuda.

During the 1940s and 1950s, Emilie wrote prose as well as poetry, and had her stories published in magazines including *The Prairie Schooner* and H.L. Mencken's *The American Mercury*. One story chosen by Mencken went on to be included in *Best American Short Stories*. The fiction I have been able to locate consists of tear sheets left in a shopping bag, and other stories I have found online or in bound volumes of periodicals. Many of the small journals that published her stories have never been indexed, so it is not possible to know how many more stories were published. Some of the tear sheets do not bear the name of the journal in which they were published. As more come to light, I will be able to expand this volume in successive printings.

The story, "Cup of Gold" existed only in a first draft, its pages unnumbered and scrambled out of order. It needed only a light editorial touch to bring it to a finished state. The short-short story, "Kite Away," was also a manuscript.

The prose poem, "From This Window," published in the *New Directions* annual in 1953, was a special favorite of Emilie's. On relaxed nights at her soirees, if the crowd was not too large, she indulged herself (and us) by reading this work in its entirety. She was unhappy that *New Directions* had published the prose-poem without full blank lines between the paragraphs, as she intended and insisted. She wanted the sense of a real pause after each item, so her intention has been honored in this volume. I have placed "Bamboo At the Grave" within prose poems as I felt it was some-where between "sketch" and "prose poem," more impressionistic than plot-driven.

Emilie's interest in writing and publishing fiction seems to have faded away by the 1970s, and many of her later narrative poems are compressed short stories, usually character portraits. It is possible that she forsook writing hundreds of stories in order to give us thousands of poems.

No matter the vessel, the art was assured. Every writer who knew her stood in awe of her ability to work day after day, year after year, seemingly without a "block." Rejections that would throw other writers into a depression just rolled off her. She typed and mailed out a dozen or more poems every day. Each day's mail contained rejection slips, acceptances, tear sheets, printed magazines with her poems in them, and, once in a great while, a tiny check. On and on and on, for four decades she had done this, untiring, unremitting. Until senility and dementia overcame her, she had the privilege of being a full-time writer. She kept herself free of romantic entanglements, her mind free from cant and religion, and never touched alcohol or drugs. She knew exactly what the Muse required, and Nature had endowed her with prodigious health.

As a New York personality and friend of poets, Emilie Glen was one of the happiest lights of Greenwich Village in what we now know to be its literary Indian Summer. Emilie Glen died at the end of 1995 and never saw a book of her own fiction. Now her time has come.

—Brett Rutherford
Pittsburgh, January 2016

(A longer version of this essay appears in Volume 1, with more biographical information about the poet, and more details about her published books and chapbooks)

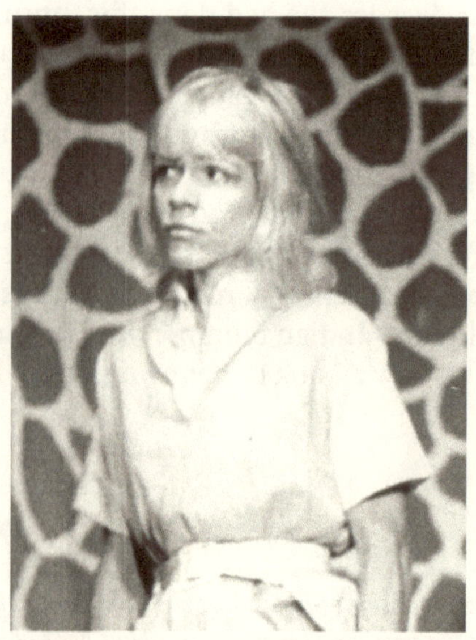

Emilie Glen in 1960, appearing in an
off-off-Broadway stage play.

FICTION

WALDRON HOLD

THERE SHE GOES, there goes Kate Waldron. Bermuda rides at sure anchor when the old islanders walk. Afternoons, Kate walked into Hamilton from Spanish Point to ride any ferry or sight-seeing boat pulling out. Always a white linen suit, mended, remended; cracked oxfords white with coral dust; hair yellow white as churned sea foam beneath a straw sailor pulpy from salt winds; rock jaw, sea-blue eye, nose a lost puppy from some non-Waldron source.

Traders, the Waldrons, of the smuggling order, back in the early 1700s when ships outsailed such formalities as customs by going through the narrows to the Flats or Mangrove Bay. Before banks and after, they hid their gold and silver in rum kegs and hollowed-out cedar beams. Buried-treasure rumors still wash in about the caves of Cooper's Island, although the more recent fortune is seeable as Waldron Hold, a terraced mansion built by Joel Waldron, Kate's uncle, on Waldron Island in the Great Sound.

Joel Waldron never did anything proper, never banked his money, kept books, nor made a proper will. He lost his only son before his eyes, saw the ship break up on the reefs in a hurricane. His ninety-seventh year, he called his nephews and nieces together, and said, "A ship can have only one captain. Same with Waldron Hold. Better a chance to win all, than nobody winning. Let's see what Tropio does." He whistled to golden-glow feathers, a black-tipped little bird in a miniature Chinese garden before a jade temple.

"Put a coin in Tropio's beak," Uncle Joel said to Kate. The bird beaked the coin, dropped it into an offering box, beaked open the temple door, and hopped back to her with a folded slip of paper, shiny white.

"Don't open it until the others draw," said Uncle Joel. "Whoever gets the fortune marked Waldron Hold wins my estate when I ship out."

A rush as of shells in surf as they unfolded their fortunes at Uncle Joel's signal. All without a pearl except Cousin Fred's.

Winner take all, so literal to Fred that no cousin has seen the inside of Waldron Hold since Tropio beaked. Three of the cousins still live in Bermuda, one moved to America, another to England.

Kate lives in a furnished room in Pembroke Parish where she has a part-time job working with the poor.

"How's my sweetheart today?" asked the ticket-taker, letting her through to the ferry dock before she scrabbled any deeper into her palmetto carryall.

She boarded the tourist boat to the Sea Gardens. The guide would exact no shillings from her; she never took up room in the glass-bottom boats, knew the Sea Gardens by heart, the plumes and fans, the fingering anemones, bulging brain stones, blue angel fish.

Boat's engine beating, waters creaming, bay breezes playful as dolphins, as they prowed out into the Great Sound. Bermuda clouds castled up from the isle rather than condescending from the sky. Sky isle, sea isle, sky sea island.

"Water like emeralds and sapphires," the woman next her was saying to her husband. "What causes all those different blues and greens? It can't be the clouds. Bermuda clouds give the water a radiance."

"Shallow and deep does it," she told her, "and the violet like great lily pads, that's caused by reefs and sea weeds. One tourist wanted to take home three bottles, one with a little of the green water, another with the blue, and another of that nice violet."

Terraces fragrant with oleanders but salted, everything salted, hibiscus, the greeters over garden walls. Among houses of pink and white coral, a few nostalgic for Italy or ranch America, when Bermuda was an isle anyone would wander the globe to find.

Wilder now, to the lone rock islands pocked as meteors. "What's happened to all your trees?" The husband's nose veined lobster, probably from eating too much of it in rich creams and sauces, as he pointed his binoculars to hills shorn as Samson.

"Cedars, the pride of our island — we lost them to the blight."

"That strong tea smell all over the island," said his wife, trying to keep her blue-tinted hair coifed in salt-sea wind. "Is it the cedars?"

"Yes, dead cedars. Monoxide caused it, some say, monoxide from too many planes and motor cars."

The boat coming to Uncle Joel's island — her heart in such flipflops whenever she neared it that she'd think something was wrong if she didn't know the strong Waldron heart, and with sea salt for blood — how could you have a stroke?

Ship house of cedars, the roof built like a ship with cedar knees to brace the corners, and great cedar rafters throughout. Past the bare cedar grove, the royal poinciana flowered in clusters like blood grapes. Cousin Fred's cabin cruiser rode at anchor — always at anchor. No sea lover like herself, even though she didn't swim too well, nor sail dinghies to victory. If she were to name her special talent it wouldn't be china painting, wouldn't be needlework, but love of the sea, Bermuda sea. Ached for Waldron as a captain for his ship. *Her* ship house, hers by right of being more like Uncle Joel than the other cousins. Many a Bermuda spinster from war, shipwreck, or lack of chances, while she had turned down land breathers, even sea followers, for not being Uncle Joel.

"See the ship-like house high up on that island?" ... a regular courser crested her tongue to, "It's mine — my ship."

Her lie hanging off their faces like a stilt-eyed crab. She hurried to the hold as fast as polite. The Waldrons were doers not talkers, never having to crouch on liar's haunches. She must get back to full height, go upside and tell the truth. The engine had stopped, tourists were climbing into the glass-bottom boats, going into their huddle over the glass to the deep-blue angel fish, sergeant majors yellow and black as Tropio beaking her a blank-sea gardens to the tourists, dark reefs to Uncle Joel watching his son die.

Sailing back to Hamilton, the husband and wife were talking to people on both sides of them, she couldn't get near to undo her lie. On the pier she caught up, "When I said Waldron Hold was mine, I meant it was in the family. I don't own it."

"Waldron Hold?" ... vacantly at her blue-white coif ... "Oh, the house on the island. You must visit it often enough to feel it's yours—" "No, that was part of the agreement when Cousin Fred—" but they were hurrying after a taxicab.

She crossed the street to Thomas Miles for a bit of cheese and biscuits to munch on the walk home. Jim Stearns tucked a gift into her carryall that St. Davidians would rather hide for themselves than sell, mullet roe more delicate than the finest caviar.

As she turned into Queen Street she saw Cousin Fred coming out of the tobacconist's, a shriveled Uncle Joel with his mother's coffee-bean eyes. Spied her, tried to unspy by lizarding behind the big old rubber tree by the library, anything to get out from under her look as if she were Uncle Joel come back to catch him burying the master's talent .... "And I was afraid and went and hid thy talent in the earth."

Cousin Fred's bride had run out on Bermuda, or on Bermuda with him. All he could do not to follow her to London town, the tide of wanting to be free of Waldron, a torrent through the narrows of his mind, a rush of waters that always piled back to the island.

Slow tided in her walk going back, by the lie about Waldron Hold being hers, almost like a black-out, words not of her speaking. Horns honked like geese behind her, never should have let them on the island.

Her house, she dwelled in it far deeper than Cousin Fred carrying it like a weight on his pinched little back. Still not Waldron to go around saying she lived in it.

She climbed to St. John's Church for a silence greater than her will.

Even here, the smell of cedar burnt it in, burnt in Waldron. She reached out the prayer book from her carryall, it turned to the usual place. "The trees of the Lord are full of sap; even the cedars of Lebanon" ... and in *Kings*, "the cedar of the house within was carved with open flowers; all was cedar; there was no stone seen."

She ate her cheese and biscuits by the side of the road in a sunset like the red shade of the poinciana, poured her thermos cup to tea like liquid cedar, spread a biscuit with a taste of the mullet roe.

As she walked on in the twilight, Bermuda, a floating island of whistlers, one whistling frog seemed to be chasing her like the ghost of Paget Sound, the pursuing bicycle bell that turned out to be Fillilo, the bird ventriloquist. Her ghost, ship's bell, Uncle Joel lifting her up to ring it — was it on a real ship or the ship's bell at Waldron Hold?

Night on this island of honeymooners like the hibiscus in the dark of unseen colors, she, the captain watchful on the bridge. No, not captain yet, not captain of Waldron. Burnt island, twin-coned from ancient volcanoes, hurricaned, wild, yet ordered — Uncle Joel. Wind-tiered, wind-seeded, grass hard come by, thirst quenched only from the skies. A snakeless Eden. No tree of knowledge for her, no nakedness, and for that one knowledge denied, all knowing, all life....

First day she trusted herself to take a truthful ride on the Sea Garden boat, she talked to no one, didn't even sit on the side of

Waldron Hold, but she couldn't keep her heart from its usual capers as they neared the island.

Nobody should lack for anything, live niggardly, by the abundant sea. With Waldron, she could be captain of her ship, not just suffered on this isle.

Clouds like the stout ribs of ships a-building, the afternoon the ticket-taker at the dock told her that Cousin Fred's counsellor, young George Atters, was trying to reach her. Rush of blood, her tan might hide. Had Fred heard about the lie? Could he take it out on her in some legal way? She hurried up to the office to get it over with.

"Good afternoon, Miss Waldron," with the accent on the *good*. Young Arters had been a pupil in her Sunday school class, and if he couldn't recite the books of the Bible, how could he know his law books?

"I have news for you, most interesting news. Fact is, Miss Waldron, your cousin is such a meticulous man of honor, so much so that he —"

"I know — I never should have said Waldron Hold was mine."

"Waldron? Yes, it's about Waldron. According to an old law, property acquired through gambling is not lawfully owned. No survivors have contested your cousin's right to Waldron Hold nor would you, but it preys —"

"Of course not. It was Uncle Joel's wish, and it wasn't gambling, it was fortune telling."

"Still, there were no proper papers, no signatures, nothing in legal order. His ownership wouldn't hold up in a court of law. We had our little conversation some years ago, but it's been haunting him all this time. He has decided to give up Waldron Hold."

"Give it up! Uncle Joel would never hear of it. Waldron must stay in the family."

"It will. He proposes to divide it among the heirs. To that purpose, he is arranging a meeting of the heirs at —"

"Uncle Joel's wish was that Waldron never be divided. 'A ship can have only one captain,' he said. Waldron Hold must have the care only a single owner can give, and I intend to uphold his wish."

She walked out of that land-locked little office down Queen Street mashed with orange seed capsules from the rubber tree, to the docks; boarded a ferry to think.

U NCLE JOEL says it clear," she told Cousin Fred at a meeting in young Atter's office. "Play a game, the winner to have Waldron. Play Uncle Joel's old favorite — croquet."

"With flamingos, no doubt —"

"Not a game of chance, but of skill, not too strenuous — croquet. Young Atters here can fix up the proper legal papers, get the seals and signatures."

Took words, a lot more words than Uncle Joel would use, to work Fred around to the croquet idea. Uncle Joel would have roared his plan in surf crash.

Day of the game dawned splendid, a regular Uncle Joel day, strong and sure; its first coppery gleams put her in mind of a certain iridescence in Uncle Joel's eyes by whale-oil lamp.

A Sally Bassett day by afternoon, a sizzler. Strange way to keep your name alive — burned as a poisoner on a burning hot day. She walked into Hamilton, stopping off to practice her swing with fallen branch and beer can.

Cousin Fred's motor boat was waiting for her. Today, no tourist deck past Uncle Joel's island, she'd climb right over the sides of high-tiding Waldron Ship, and win.

The old whale trying-pot still at the foot of the ladder-like steps, the anchors from two of his ships that went down off the reefs.

Many of the cedars had been cleared away, nursery spindles of another breed planted in their place. "Rather have blighted cedars than no cedars at all," she told Fred, "they're Bermuda, her ships and rafters."

"Even Uncle Joel couldn't have prevented the blight."

"He'd have thought of something."

The royal poinciana red-lighted the lawn gleaming with wickets. The imported turf couldn't stand the sun like wiry Bermuda grass. A new croquet set, paint perfect, unreal as cinecolor. "Where's Uncle Joel's set?" ... only a smooth worn handle felt good to the grip.

"Too battered. Some mallets are ground down worse than others. It wouldn't be fair."

Five players in all, the other four in fidgets of waiting: a young second cousin from the States, his sandpiper wife trying to keep their three youngsters off the croquet grounds; Cousin Ellen, who could wield a mean mallet, her son eyeing Waldron's possibilities as a hotel enterprise; Cousin Eli whose name in the Bermuda news was always coupled with sportsman, mostly for his dinghy racing; Cousin Lewis, now of Manchester, who used to knock her ball to hell and gone just as she neared the goal post. More of Uncle Joel in him, still his wife, his son and daughter, their children about them, were there on the lawn half wanting him to lose such an encumbrance.

Quite an assortment of grandchildren for young Atters to keep a legal distance from the playing field just as she had been armed back from grown-up games ... had drowsed in the red shade of the poinciana to the lullaby leaves, silk skirts about the lawn.

She chose a red-banded mallet as always, had to have red to win, used to race Uncle Joel for the red, he never treated her as a child but as a menacing rival.

Uncle Joel, the sixth player today, at her arm when she hit the ball through the first three wickers to a good position at the center, the fallen petals of the poinciana pointing her path across the lawn.

Cousin Ellen sent her ball through the first two wickets in such a desperate drive it went off course for the third.

Lewis, in his old aim, shot through two wickets and into her ball with one stroke till she could almost feel her hair swinging down her back again, buttons cutting into her instep.

Young John went farthest in the first play, even ahead of Eli — fifth wicket.

In a drive to stop young John, she hit so hard, her ball spun wild across the namby-pamby grass.

An even game to the first stake. Cousin Eli, hoorayed by his young ones, started for the home goal. Back to girl giggles, Cousin Ellen turned unladylike long enough to roquet Eli's ball, and send it across the field to shouts and hoots, Ellen's grandchildren in cartwheels.

Lewis wired her own ball, making a shot through the wicket so impossible that she roqueted Ellen's ball, sent it rolling. "Foul strike," young Atters called out as she poised her mallet.

"What do you mean, foul strike? I roqueted fair and square."

"But you're taking another shot. You can't have another shot when you've sent your opponent's ball out of bounds."

Youngsters began jumping out on the playing field. "Back," salivaed Cousin Fred, "back — back."

Foul and all, she recovered in her next two turns. Cousin Eli was creeping up meanwhile, scoring quiet points while the others took croquet. She disposed of him in a neat swing that had the youngest of them sucking in their breaths, sent Lewis's ball back to Eli's.

Lewis roqueted his way back to her just as she was in position for the center wicket, missed.

With little chance of winning, Ellen went roquet wild, the way she used to when her curls were hanging, knocked her out of position, sent young John away, dispatched Lewis.

Recovering, Lewis went through the third to last wicket ahead of her, right into position for the final two. Young John missed his chance to stop Lewis.

Up to her, must roquet him all the way from the center of the field. *Joel, Joel, steady* ... youngsters dancing like sunspots .... "Stand still, or clear out" ... could be Uncle Joel's surf boom, the way they statued.

She swung — hit — sent him, not too far, not out of bounds, roqueted young John, roqueted Ellen, went through the third last wicket, and into a somewhat wired position for the final two. From across the field, Lewis lifted his mallet, prolonged the stance, the aim — swung. Missed.

Poinciana petals a confused dance before her eyes in the way of the wire gleam. She looked out to the sea in blue dance, and back to her ball in sure red band, measured her distance with narrowed eyes, heard Uncle Joel's *Swing easy*, cleared one, cleared two, hit the stake ... Captain of Waldron Ship.

Voices boiling around her like the waters of Devil's Hole .... Why give Waldron to the end of a life? Let them think it. She was good for twenty-seven Joel years yet; she would outlive a lot of these weak stalks.

Young John's little boy ran to keep up with her steps as she took a quick climb to what was left of Uncle Joel's cedar grove where he used to tell her stories of the sea ... the boy's questions fast as their climb .

"Were Bermuda ships made of the very same cedars as the houses?"

"Yes, and stools were made of whale bone, an early school on St. David's had nothing but whale bone stools and lamps of whale and turtle oil."

"Did you see ships smashed in a hurricane from up here, Aunt Kate?"

"Why, I've seen Bermuda stormed by waves like great white-winged horses, uprooting trees, shaking houses, tearing away roofs, the very cloudbursts salted with skyward spray. I've seen men caught in a broken topsail that was rushing them out to sea —"

"And did it? Were they drowned?"

"Miraculous as the waves that washed a seaman overboard only to wash him back on deck again, rescuers at the bottom of a cliff, held out a Pole to them, they caught hold, and were pulled to safety."

"Wow!" ... The boy had missed out on the stout-timbered Waldron build, the sea eye, his brown, earth brown, except for the far gaze of the crow's nest.

A bit of legal this and legal that, a sea-bag of belongings to tote, and she was Captain of Waldron Ship. Breathing in the salt cedars, she treasure-hunted among the stuffs of the seven seas, the ivories, the jades, the rocks and minerals, shells and fans and shawls, hammered gold of the Incas, cloisonné, intaglio, tapestries, laces, woodcarving, and the temple garden with its new Tropio.

AS CAPTAIN of Waldron, she had precious little time for the poor of Pembroke Parish — money and goods, but no self, when that was what they needed most, somebody caring; and what she needed most. They were her family.

No taste for luxuries, she liked the hard seat, the hard mattress, the simple foods. That's how she kept well. Too blubber-soft with servants to all but sneeze for you. Hard living, sea living, Bermuda's strength, like the hard-fibered vegetation.

As a captain working right along with her crew, her walks were confined to Waldron isle, her rides to sea were few, even with cabin cruiser, sailboat, motor boat, docked below.

Counsellors, she was never free of them, her counsellor, somebody else's counsellor. More desk work administering Waldron Hold than on the job she had given up. As a working captain she had to know waxes, polishes, insecticides, preventives, preservatives, restoratives, had to treat leathers, polish precious metals, buck the stubbornness of materials, what they would and would not do. Waldron began being heavy, began being house.

Joel knew, he knew when he called Waldron *Hold*, not *Ship*, knew that Bermuda is the ship, Waldron the hold, and who wants to stay in the hold?

Bermuda had always been hers until she tried to captain Waldron Hold.

An afternoon when Bermuda Ship seemed to have hoisted anchor, to be tiding along in the tourmaline sea, she walked in on young Atters. "I'm giving up Waldron Hold. Make it proper and legal, but turn it over to the boy John under the guardianship of his parents, or however you do it — a clause for Uncle Joel, of course, about not dividing the property. I want nothing."

Walked out of young Atter's office and down to Front Street, berries of the rubber tree bursting underfoot.

"Hello, sweetheart," said the ticket-taker, letting her through. Timed it right, the coral-reef boat about to pull out. She would sail right on past Waldron, never saying it had been hers, right on past to the open sea.

[Prairie Schooner, Fall 1956]

ASK ME

BROOKLYN has its gypsy king, Manhattan its royalty, but they're tufted titmice compared to the cap-crested king of the Ramble, Milton Vogel.

Rock-wild, the Ramble up in Central Park is not much bigger than a bread crust dropped from a helicopter gnatting Manhattan towers. What happens in the Ramble, Spring and Fall, is the surprise in the crackerjack, a ruby in the cement mix.

Up from the Gulf of Mexico, Central America, the Argentine, up North with the South wind, back with the North wind, flying the gourmet route for bug and berry dainties, birds make a motel of the Ramble above the boating lake, fly miles of cement, skim monoxide skyscrapers to put down at its green-open doors.

Striped cap on backwards, handkerchief hung Arab against the sun and sweat, the bird-little man holds walking court. Bird-black eyes siding a parakeet face dart after birds as birds' eyes after food.

Milt won his rock throne, his leafy scepter, in the battle of the binoculars, by outlensing all other birdwatchers. He never carries a field guide into the field, but he does own Peterson's for home study, and books enough on birds to be legendary in his lore, People lense his coming, so they can watch birds better. Gifts to the bird-king are sumptuous — bird prints on silk and rice paper, bird carvings in ivory and jade, anything bird.

Birders inviting him to dinner or the theater, he refuses. Only here is he king — here his only oxygen. He closes a lashless eye against anything indoors, eye feathered with lines from squinting after the little fellows.

Milt's birdwatch day begins at 4:45 when he eats a bird breakfast in his furnished room two blocks and a half from the Ramble. A widower, his two married sons far from Manhattan, he gave himself the fiftieth birthday present of selling Vogels, his photographic equipment store, and is living so-so on the proceeds.

One must be punctual to the birds. Just before sunrise he enters the Park at Eighty-sixth Street, a dozen blocks up from the entrances of most birdwatchers, in order to maintain his divine right of discovering the rare ones before his subjects arrive. Willing to bring them to the vicinity of some of his finds, he still keeps himself somewhat supernatural by saving certain coves and ravines, the baseball field above the weather tower, for birds that probably will appear only on his own Life List, such as a cowbird in among the starlings, a long-eared owl, a snowy egret.

King of high birding standards, he never cheats. What he says he sees, he sees. Of course he might flush a mourning warbler or a hooded to flight before anyone can sight what he saw.

Let birders lie or falsify their Life List, and he will put them to route with ridicule. Along about eight the professional men and business executives, the ten o'clock deskers, come to lense a few with Milt's help, before the office presses them *duck*. With them his approach to birding is as professional as theirs to their work.

Secretaries and such, birding on their slim-skeined lunch hour, he treats to a bit more showmanship; flashes his lense to a sense of birds behind every leaf; gives them a quickness of thrushes, warblers, finches; sends them off to their office exits with promises of a yellow chat or a white-crowned sparrow on the bowling green.

House ladies bird in the afternoon, seeking out his patience in seeing that they see what he sees. Mostly men come hunting with their field glasses. Certain acrobatics are required to climb rocks, descend into ravines. Neck and shoulders must be strong for the treetop stretch. Muggers on the stuff have learned the value of binoculars.

Birders are such a watchful lot, muggers can seldom attack from behind. Even so, the king carries a vicious fish-hook wrapped in a paper bag, fish-hook from the days when he first turned to birding.

Mid married years he would lock up his photographic shop, and go deep-sea fishing. Little jewel birds he didn't know as warblers then would come to rest on his fishing boat, after a flight of thousands of miles, he read later, the tiny ones so exhausted he had to net some of them out of the ocean. No welfare state for the plucky little birds cemented away from their green, blinded by the show-off lights of tall buildings, airways thick with planes, killed by DDT.

In the wingless still of the Forty-second Street library, he took wing, reading about the mysteries of bird flight North, flight South. A Bronx boy up out of the cement, crated into an apartment, was in wonderment that little flying jewels stop over in Central Park; that just about all the birds in the color plates find their way past seas of cement, their minute eyes spotting what there is of city green beneath the towers; that eagles live on skyscrapers.

His winter palace — his alone. Not a birdwatcher, not one. He had his cardinal family to feed, his tufted titmice, even a winter wren. A chickadee would light on his hand for peanut bits. Jays blued the snow. Of course, he couldn't go along with their nest-marauding habits much as he tried not to moralize about the birds.

This day of May, with fox sparrows about, the white-throats, and a white-crown sighted only by him, pines and palms, the rest of the warblers but a South wind away, Milt lensed a bereted bone of a man pointing about the upper Ramble at six in the morning.

Lensing with him down to the cove, Milt put him to the test. "What have you got there?"

"Semi-palmated plover."

"So you have."

Binoculars well worn, more so than his own, higher powered Zeiss from World War I. "My Father's Father's Father's. He started me birding up in the Maine woods when I was little more than a bean shoot." Where but in New England would they breed such skeletons? He was scribbling more than a Life List — whole sentences in a spiral notebook.

"Your Life List seems to be taking on the proportions of a log book."

"Something like that. I'm covering the birds of Central Park for a book Dutton will be publishing next Spring. I also write a nature column for a Long Island newspaper. Name is Bryce Cramer —" intoned First Family.

Well, Bryce was scooping no news from him. Before he could beak at his brain with that dowitcher nose, Milt went down Ramble to where his people would be arriving; dropped his news like the remains of a well eaten clam, "Saw a semi-palmated plover."

"Where — where?" ... Crowd starting up about him "Hey, wait a minute, Milt" ... "What's to see today?" "Saw a bird I can't identify, sort of messy in his colorings" ... "Quick — quick — what have I got?"... like the excitement at the coming of the lead onto the stage ... "Think I spotted a painted bunting."

"A painted bunting? Not likely."

Bryce rattling his skeleton. "He's right. I saw a painted bunting earlier — positive identification —" Not here to listen — learn — but to talk — teach.

"You didn't let me finish. Not likely, but anything can happen in the Ramble, as witness the small red bird that turned out to be a summer or Western tanager."

"Well, I'm off to the Natural History Museum to study the skins. Too many questionables lately."

That's all Bryce cared for, the little jewel ones, callously willing to thumb through their dead feathers. Why, when Milt glassed them on the South wind, he flew with them.

By Thursday, the feather preener bereted above a number of followers, most of them stolen from him. Just find something special, and they would hop hop back. Only the usual flew across his crystal. The faithful cooed over his finding of pines and palms; others crossed over to see what Bryce was lensing, They were forgetting all Milt did for their birding joy. He was the one who fought it out with the Park department to leave ground cover for the birds, plant the right trees for food, and when they neglected the drain pipes, he got down on his knees, and cleared out the orifice with his own hands to let the water flow crystal free for the little drinkers.

Tomorrow he would spot such a rare one that Bryce would belly-crawl over to his group,

Morning brought only the usual. He edged his sparse group across the brook from a bird. Bryce's pigeons were cooing about. "A brewster warbler —" he claimed, that sun-burst hybrid of a gold-wing and a blue-wing.

"Wait a minute — just a minute — from where I stand that's no brewster, it's a female golden-wing."

His people crossing the brook back to him, "Milt's right — he's always right."

Bryce twigged off alone through the woods.

That was the lunch-hour crowd. The afternooners had to be won all over again. Time to come up with the Brazilian cardinal he knew was in the ravine, escaped from some pet shop. Just as he had his glasses trained on him, Bryce had to bound up like a branch in the face, to mouth in unison, "Escapee."

"Yes, a Brazilian cardinal." In the effect of naming the bird, Milt winged off into the woods too fast for any followers to catch up.

Beret-head's exact naming of trees and bushes fooled many into thinking he knew that much more about the birds. A couple of sessions with Miss Pritchett and he would know as much as Bryce's Father's Father's Father taught him.

Call-notes and bird-songs, you could never have enough knowledge of them, although he was already beyond Bryce's dried-cod ear. Supernatural, that's what his faithful thought of his hearing.

Come tomorrow — a rare one — but tomorrow came in rain. The Ramble his alone — Bryce not the type to slog around with wet feet and no audience. He breathed in with the South wind, the smell of spiced woods, wet rocks, the lake, salt smell of a sea not far. A prairie warbler hopped right out onto the path, eyeing him through his black spectacles, rain-polished to a brighter yellow. Goldfinches chased through the willows. A scarlet tanager wrapped a dead branch in red velvet. Hermit thrushes followed him about.

Letting his glasses hang, he enjoyed the unmagnified tininess of ruby-crowned kinglets, brown creepers, black-and-whites along the bark, a chickadee to his hand for peanuts. Why, he almost began to feel feathered himself.

A warbler he couldn't identify without his binoculars; could it be — dare he breath it even to himself — a Swainson's warbler — never before sighted here that he knew of. A Swainson's, and no one to witness.

Sun of Sunday, the watchers crazing their lenses around like Sunday drivers, he sneaked off to the upper Ramble after a Swainson's that must have taken off in the night.

At risk of a trampled Ramble he told his followers about his find. Bryce skeletoned over to him in the late afternoon. "Rumor has it, you saw a Swainson's — " said in his Harvard voice, or was it Princeton?

"Right-o," Milt came back British.

"Any witnesses?"

"That's a bloody insult. I don't need witnesses. If I said I saw an emu, I saw an emu."

"You're a capital birdwatcher. It's just that —"

"Then mention me in your book when you say a Swainson's was sighted."

"Sorry — I can't report hearsay. I must see the bird. However, if I sight it, if it fits into book or column, I may mention that you were first to lense the bird."

"Thank you — thank you, mightily — oh great friend of the feathered — "

"Truth is, I'm suspicious of anyone too sure. Those who know are more apt to say *I don't know*."

"That excludes you." If the words were a club, he would have knocked Bryce off the rock.

Former followers crashed over from beret-head during bird-wave days, only to fast-beak after his Life List. On to their hit-and-run, he kept his Life List hidden as his fish-hook. Without a look at his List they paid no more attention to him than to a common sparrow, a weaver finch.

Even the rare fly-through avoided him these June days, or the acids of hating beret-head darked his lense.

Into the twilight of a blackpoll day, the black and white end of the warbler wave. Only he and Bryce were still lensing. Both climbed the same rock, trying to make out whether a certain wren was long billed or short billed.

"Looks like a long bill," he said, more to himself than to Bryce,

"No — no — not necessarily — the eye line isn't all that white—"

"Are you trying to discredit me?" Ached to pop him like a dried seaberry. "I have yet to arrive at a conclusion. The cap appears to be rusty —"

Footing after a better view, he bumped into Bryce so hard they both fell off the rock, binoculars in better condition than his right wrist. The wren still in the reeds. With his left hand he almost focused a rusty cap. Bryce, knocked out in the shore ooze, was past speculating.

Waiting for the ambulance he had time to make positive identification, just about established the white eyeline when the wren winged across the lake.

Both were treated in the same emergency room: Milt for a sprained wrist and assorted bruises; Bryce for a broken collar-bone and contusions. All the while Milt apologized for an accident he wasn't sure was an accident.

It would be a birding while before Bryce would limp over to the Ramble. He, himself, was there at dawn, an ace bandage about his wrist so tight it interfered with lensing and rock climbing.

Before the month was out, Bryce rattled his bones over to the Ramble, a walking bunch of bandages, like the invisible man, his neck too stiff for lensing above eye level, dead center.

Everyone flocking like starlings to chatter about their bandages; could almost read their lips as they speculated on how he and Bryce must have locked binoculars in deadly combat. If they nerved to ask him what happened, of course he would call it an accident however loud his mind shouted "no accident."

One dawn he thought was his own, he lensed Bryce in leather and metal collar point — nosing after a bird for his obscure column.

On a log across the lake — snow-bank of white — not possible. No such bird had ever whited these shores, sunned it with an orange pouch. A white pelican more at home in the West and the Caribbean than in an Eastern skyscraper city.

Pelican too huge for beret-head's finicking eyes. He had yet to spot it. Milt trained his glasses on a branch farthest from the pelican.

"A find, I presume."

"Blue-wing without a tail."

"Without a tail? Where?"

"Five o'clock — the ironwood tree. Flew. If we climbed that rock —"

"No, thank you."

With the arrival of the doctors, lawyers, late-desk executives, hookey players, he beaked up "What's new?" with "A pelican."

"Pelican? Sure you didn't misspeak?"

"No, and I don't drink. A pelican."

Bryce stealing it — "He's right, this time. I noted the pelican at 5:17. Milt arrived at 5:26, but we were too busy chasing his alleged blue-wing without a tail to discuss the pelican."

What that dowitcher didn't know was that he had already phoned the story into The New York Times. It would be front-page of the second section of tomorrow's paper.

Times photographers were already flashing the pelican when every birdwatcher in the Ramble climbed the ridge across from the great one as if they were conquering Indians. Phone calls alerted the absent. Lunch-hour people left their desks early, the morning people stayed on through with the afternoon people.

Bypassing Bryce's "sighted at 5:17," reporters interviewed Milt for a feature story as King birder of Central Park Ramble.

As soon as the feature story appeared in the Times, his followers were all his, leaving Bryce to bird by his stiff-collared self, or join the group as one of his followers. The Linnean Society conferred an honorary membership — the Audubon magazine wrote him up — not just for the pelican, but for his devotion to the birds.

Beret-head showed less often. Last heard from by picture postcard to Miss Pritchett, he had changed his *Birds of Central Park* for *Birds of Central America*. Hmmm — field open.

His people were coming to him with everything they spotted— "Phone it into the Times, Milt — phone it in."

BEAUTY IS IN THE BONE

THEY WORKED into the November darkness to take away the look of a doctor's suite from their new apartment. Marion put complexion-flattering bulbs in the sockets, to turn the former examining room into her Mother's idea of a rose petal boudoir.

"Landlords still do very little for their tenants. Don't they know we won't be having an apartment shortage much longer? Look at these floors, not scraped and sanded, not even —"

"You're not in your parqueted suite at the Carleton House, Mother."

"At least we have a private entrance, and we're just off Park Avenue. When I think how you were living after your divorce, Marion, that furnished room near the Natural History Museum, and I in a room at the Weylin after your father died. When I think what little we were able to salvage from your Father's estate, I can't help wishing you had let Albert make the settlement he could well afford."

"You know how I feel about that, Mother. Unless there are children, a man should not be penalized for no longer loving you."

"I don't understand, I thoroughly don't understand — a girl with your advantages being every way shy, even money shy. You could put your geological training to commercial use just as Albert did, discovering oil for a big company. Instead, you putter around as an underpaid assistant in that dingy Museum of Natural History."

"I'm not going to be used as a hound dog sniffing out oil. I'm a chemical geologist. My job is to analyze rocks and minerals. Oh mother, let's not get on our differences at the start of living together. Here I am thirty-three years old, and —"

"Let's not begin with age reminders, Marion. You'd better be twenty-six, and never breathe fifty-four around me. I'm forty-five."

"You can pass for younger than you are, Mother, but I looked *in my thirties* before I left my early twenties."

"That's just it, you have one of those indefinite faces. You could be any age."

"Well, thanks. Why is it you are hyper-tactful with everyone but me?"

"The idea is to assess what you have to work with."

"Nothing to assess. Even with like interests I couldn't hold Albert. I was so afraid of losing him that I did lose him. Guess I was too tense with him, worked too hard at being what he wanted, someone more like you, Mother."

"You won't believe this, but I've had to work at being considered the third generation beauty. My grandmother always said 'true beauty is repose,' but if I didn't keep turning my head, everyone would note that the two halves of my face are not well matched, I need right three-quarters or profile to be at my best. My mother and grandmother never needed fashion nor any sort of illusion, and it was easier for them to become legends in village and small city than for me in an international setting."

Mother was at the mirrored door, the triple image, three generations of Saunders beauties — Mother, Mother's mother, Mother's mother's mother — beauty based on bone structure, proud planes that outsculptured age. Mother's mother had a nose of such excruciating perfection that the faintest stir of features would break down the delicate bridge. The auburn waves of hair that persisted in three generations, also persisted into age without turning, eyes the petaled brown that goes with auburn — except Mother. Her eyes a delphinium blue that she passed along to her as faded denim, hair browned down, tired bone structure that with all her embroidered organdies as a child, gave her a waif look. She had felt less wretched listening to "You don't take after your Mother," than to the searchers after fourth generation beauty, "You have your Mother's long fingers," "her slim ankles," "eyes, her blue in some lights."

With her gifted touches, it took Mother only a few days to turn the suite into a jewel box for auburn hair and blue eyes, supposed also to warm her own pallor.

Mother tried to redecorate their persons, too, with beauty treatments, shampoos, facials, experiments in makeup. Mother couldn't afford the former beauty round, but she had carried over diets and exercises from costly salon courses. Couldn't help purring awhile in the sun of Mother's attentions — hair brushed to faint luster, fingers working at tensed nerve centers, words of caring, "Marion dear, you'll get frown lines reading in that light" "Stop digging your knuckles into your cheek, you're hollowing it out" "Why the apologetic stoop? Stand up to your height."

All this, Mother regarded as being partner in the business of finding second mates.

As they exercised before the mirror, her Mother's fifty-four glowed younger than her thirty-three. "Mother, what's the use? This isn't doing any more for me than smocking used to do. Why crawl up the wall and pedal the air when I'm nothing but bones —"

"Exercises do more than reduce, they round out, redistribute what weight you do have, improve posture, whip up the blood."

As Mother became more involved with her suitors, and she, in her geological research on the book she hoped would tum out like Rachel Carson's *Sea*, they came and went like the tourists they used to be when Dad's business took them across Europe, the jewel box no more living together than a suite in Antwerp or Copenhagen. Child of a beautiful Mother, meant being warded off from silks and coifs, powders and pleats.

With the skill she had developed as a minor relation of a major family, Mother planned her mate stratagem. To save enough to be seen at fashionable restaurants, Mother would dine at home on scraps from the icebox that once held drugs and biotics. She went forth only in style, turned down all but direct result invitations, and then proceeded with indirection. Out of all this, Mr. Ely, multimillionaire widower, President of many a board, emerged as Mother's new husband.

Mother left little behind when she moved to his Park Avenue suite with two of his four daughters, just a couple of empty hatboxes, and the scent of her creams and lotions.

"Ingratiate yourself," Mother said from her briar rose sofa in the new powder blue living room. "Alvin is lonely, most very rich men are lonely, they can trust so few friendships. You can be a daughter to him."

"With four daughters already? The two with him now make me feel backstairs."

"It's up to you to win his affections. I can't do it for you. You know how suspicious rich men can be. I have charge accounts everywhere, but little ready cash. He must never be allowed to think that I married him hoping he would also take care of you. Since I signed a long term lease, I can still pay your rent, and that's about all."

"I have my museum job, it may not be enough to pay the rent, but if the book works out —"

"Take an interest in his collection of toy banks, they're almost as old as some of your rocks, and very amusing, the monkey that holds out its hat for coins, and the squirrel who eats them. He might, just might, have your book published, see to the promotion, everything —"

"Mother, I want a publisher to *want* to publish my book."

TRIPS ABROAD, months at one or another of Mr. Ely's country homes, kept down Mother's look-ins to a relief and a loneliness. Good to be among rocks again, the story of ages instead of the chatter of minutes, a story that quickened for her the words of Genesis, "and the earth was without form and void; and darkness was upon the face of the deep."

Holidays, it was *Poor Marion*, until she had to pretend gala plans. "You're such a recluse since you started that book, Marion. You seem to think that since your marriage to Albert didn't work out, no marriage will."

Mother, who considered all stress a threat to beauty, tried to remain detached when she had to phone her at three one morning, pains so knotting violent that she could hardly hold the phone. "We mustn't panic," said her Mother, "it's probably a bit of indigestion."

"No, it's a — a lot more serious, Mother. Hurry—" She knew nothing more until she opened her eyes to a hospital room. The doctor told her later that the gastrointestinal attack was so severe, she would have died that night if her Mother had not hurried her to the hospital.

"Your Mother has taken the room right next to yours," the nurse said.

"What's wrong? Is she —"

"Nothing at all. She has decided she needs a few days of reconditioning. Her beauty secrets don't come out of a jar, — she knows looks depend on health."

Wrapped in fever, she could hear the comings and goings in Mother's room. Sometimes she had the overflow — flowers, colognes, dusting powders, chic books, visitors.

In the solarium a day or so before they left the hospital, she met someone on her own. The first afternoon they talked until the

October warmth of the glass went to mauve dusk starred by river boats.

An older man, fifty-six, with interesting bone structure like Mother's, a bit too skeletal, his eyes the darker for hair the yellow white of a churned up surf. In their sun-glassed talks, he told her about his metalwork, and in the way of American business men, confided his art love as a guilty secret. A manufacturer of industrial machinery, he said he had no business living back in the Craft Guilds with his chasing, enameling, planishing.

The day of his leaving he told her, "I'm going to Bermuda to convalesce. I'll look you up as soon as I return."

"You and — your wife?"

"I lost my wife a little over a year ago. I have a son at prep school, and two married daughters."

"While you're convalescing, you may find you like working in metals so much that you'll —"

"Oh, there's a bit of the artist in every business man, but it can't take over."

"Why not?"

Letters brought them closer together than a month of meetings. He was all hers for the space of a letter, doubt ruled out at the borders. One small square unfolded great like one of those mammoth valentines. Whenever it rained at night she would look out on the street lamp planishing the asphalt to a copper shield that might be his.

Mother lost her husband while Wayne was in Bermuda, a blood clot to the brain as he was addressing a luncheon meeting. Rushing spring with a maline puff of a hat, and delaying winter with her golden mutation mink, Mother moved back, squadroned by hat-boxes, matching luggage in her particular blue. She brought a few pieces of furniture from the Park Avenue suite, an inlaid table of rosewood and mother-of-pearl, Chinese lamps a trifle outsize for this room, royal Copenhagen porcelains and Danish silver. Again she decorated to a jewel box. Mother, with her befriending bone structure, still a jewel, hair auburn without art. Her own hair greying.

"Your rent has been frozen so low for this address," Mother said, "that we can't afford to move." Auburn radiance even in her tones. "Of course we have quite a bit more to live on, but that money can go into improvements. Everything except a few securities my husband gave me, is tied up in litigation. You should have seen the procession of lawyers with dispatch cases full of holdings. His estate may not be settled for years, meantime I must pick up my life."

"Where can I work on my book, do you suppose?"

Mothers' answer was to have the wall knocked out, the apartment extended to the garden court beyond a study decorated in forest greens and browns so right for meditation that she sat there as self-conscious as she used to be with Albert.

The little jeweled bird was already poised for the take-off. Perhaps this time, she, herself would be the first.

Azaleas crimsoned the garden, ailanthus leaves were new red, when Wayne wrote that he was on his way to her. Mother helped to dress her for his coming, makeup pink shell, hair trembling on the edge of a wave, grey blue chiffon misting away angles.

Without seeming to include herself in the preparations, Mother emerged the auburn sun. Too many had been drawn more to the family portrait than to the daughter.

Mother had a moment to arrange the portrait, adjusting folds and waves, before Wayne stood in the doorway almost startled, looking from her to Mother. His gauntness still there, fibered into tan. His height seemed to stoop before this jewel box of a waiting room.

"Would you like to see the study Mother decorated for me?"

Mother could come and go with her new beaux as long as the garden belonged to her and Wayne.

"When am I going to see the metal work you did in Bermuda?"

"I have a copper pen tray almost ready for you, an undersea fancy.

With the work that's piled up at the office, it's about all I'll manage for some time. I would like to have a go at your delicate modeling even though I'm not too good at hammering out portraits."

"Sure you don't mean Mother? She's the one with the fine bone structure."

"If you see with — well I won't say the artist's eye in reference to me — you would know that your face has fascinating planes."

Mother stayed up past her beauty sleep to talk about both their evenings. "Tonight I incline more to Wilbur Clarkson than Paul

Sievers. Wayne is thoroughly delightful, but isn't he rather old for you?"

"Oh no, Mother, we're so — well, so comfortable together."

"With his three children, you would probably wind up like me— in litigation. Just what kind of an industrialist is he?"

"Mill machinery. His true interest is metal work, he —"

"Oh, it's good when they have their hand in more than one corporation. Is it a manufacturing process like that double cracking whatever it is?"

"No, Mother, no — art metal work — chasing silver, etching copper — I'm encouraging him to —"

"Oh, they all have these half buried art ideas. You can't give into them. What if your father had gone off and joined a glee club because he was always looking back on his college travels with his glee club, or what if your stepfather had walked out on his director-ates to collect toy banks? You read what happened when Gauguin gave into his art impulse. He threw over his family."

THE AFTERNOON of her birthday, she came back from researching at the Natural History Museum grimed from trays of rocks. They started up at her from out the shadows, Mother, Wayne, "Happy birthday" ... "Happy birthday." Wayne held out a silver wrapped package, copper flashing the tissue.

"It would take a more practised metal worker to do either one of you. It's a composite, really, of you both."

Mother turned portrait at the tea service in one of her hostess gown fancies of creamed satin.

"If you'll excuse me," she said after rushing too many words into Mother's easy silences; ran to her typewriter, tears a locust swarm trying to break through.

No longer certain which one he came to see, she would retreat to her study on his visits. At first he would start up to follow her, then accustomed to her fits of work, he would stay behind with Mother.

"We think you work too hard," Mother said to her one evening, "that rock book always on your mind. "*We think* — like Mother and Father as she held out a demitasse to her with no young hand, night creamed, night gloved, structured, but old, loose skinned old.

Whenever Wayne arranged an evening with her alone, she was sure it was because Mother was with Paul or Wilbur. "I don't know," he said at the door after the theater, "we seem to have lost what we had in the sunroom, the letters."

"It wasn't enough, I guess."

"I suppose I'm too old for you."

No, oh no — afraid an inner cry so intense might burst through to his hearing. This his out, she must give him his out.

A winter afternoon that plummeted to windy dark, she came in to hear their whispered stirrings in the lightless room, crept out as if she had found them — found them — *unthinkable*.

She walked down Madison Avenue, its steamy windows of flower shops, inpetaling; went into a movie trying to care what happened to the vista-vision people; came out to such a wind that she burrowed her hands in the red-toned sealskin Mother had passed along to her after a few wearings.

She signaled a bus, rode until the driver said, "Everybody out," at the Battery, took another one uptown, trying to ride the pain away, look it away, out the window, moving now through areas of wretchedness.

The bus went to the squalid end of its run. "Last stop, lady," said the driver.

She took an empty bus back — few people in the streets, dog walkers mostly, shops blacked out or night lighted, everywhere the doleful neon a watch in the night.

A light from their apartment jagged the grille-work across the sidewalk when she turned into her street.

"Marion, child, where have you been?" Wayne's voice fathering. "You shouldn't worry your Mother like this."

"Is it inconceivable that I might stay out late? You make evenings so short, Mother, with your beauty sleep."

Old, she looked old, one worrisome night and she was a wrinkled shell of age. Should have worried her into her years long ago.

Mother waited until a number of facials later to sit in June pink of a February twilight, and say, "We've given this much thought, Wayne and I. We believe that we are right for each other, and we plan to marry in March, as soon as he comes back from his business trip. With him for a husband, I'll be able to do everything for you. You're already a daughter to him."

Mother's tones belling along ... "too old for you, dear ... someone your own age ... wish I had your young years, what I wouldn't make of them ... you're too much of a recluse, both of us agree ..." Jeweled song bird, three generations lovely, three generations of beauty in the bone.

LOAN OF THE BRITANNICA

H ER DAUGHTER-IN-LAW was pointin' like an arch over them books, shovin' 'em in too tight for their good, and goin' on about there bein' no room .... "not for two encylopedias, Mother Burridge, not both the Americana and the Britannica."

"The Britannica, did you say? Could I just travel my eye over it?"

No call to hand her the book upside down like she couldn't read or somethin', just a poor immigrant from Lancashire. What did these Americans know about the English school system where you learned more in grammar school than her son was gettin' under the G.I. Bill? Maybe her speech was a bit the worse for livin' with her husband so long, but she knew her English grammar right enough.

"Charles *would* win the Americana in an essay contest," said her daughter-in-law, "right while we're in the thick of paying off the six hundred owed on the Britannica."

"I couldn't have the loan of it, could I?"

"Why, that would solve our storage problem nicely."

"Ya know, I have a hankerin' for this kind o' book. I had the makins' of a teacher only my father wouldn't let me accept a scholarship that would've meant givin' up his whiskey to pay my expenses. That's somethin' I never got over, I guess —" Her hand on the slippery-cool page was takin' her back to some early reader, and beyond the pitchers she was seein' the old school-room with her own scrubby self at the inked-up desk.

"This ain't no double talk is it?" she asked her daughter-in-law. "I can have the encyclopedia, can't I — the loan of it, I mean?"

"Why, of course you can. You're really doing us a favor."

"Then I'll go put it in my suitcase."

"It? The one volume? There are twenty-four in all, you know."

"Oh, I didn't have no idea. I dass'n't ask for the loan of twenty-four. Besides, I couldn't tote 'em all the way to Meadville, New York, in my suitcase."

"Of course not, Mother Burridge. We'll send them along."

"Which set am I gettin' the loan of — the Britannica?"

"Why not, since the Americana fits our shelves and the Britannica doesn't?"

"Bein' British and all, there's something about it bein' the Britannica—" Britannica — *Encylopaedia Britannica* — it had a grand staircase sound, the ring of empire ....

She'd need a fine bookcase. Her husband could drive her up to Buffalo for them unpainted shelves they had at Sears and Roebuck's.

All the way to Meadville with the countryside whizzin' past the train winda, she tried to hold onto the pitcher of anything as elegant as the Britannica in her egg crate of a settin' room. Not a stick of furniture would be worth an auction if they was to die sudden, and it would all be crowdin' around the Britannica like folks before Buckingham Palace.

With Hal workin' overtime at the plant it was days before he could drive her to Sears and Roebuck's. When she asked the clerk what size bookcase would just fit the Britannica, the dumb-head asks, "What is it — how big a book?" "It's no *it*," she told him, "it's *them* — twenty-four volumes in all, not countin' the year book."

Nothin' was tall enough, not even the sectionals. Shelves for her Britannica had to be custom built like a fine motor car.

Cream color, she decided for the paint. That set the salesgirl off in a vomit of honey-dew, champagne, water lily, endive. "Cream," she kept tryin' to get in, "just plain cream." And you didn't just pick up a brush no more and start paintin'; you had to rub 'er down and fill 'er up, put on under-coats and over-coats, use this, that, and the other brush, or spray it, squirt it, roller it — all supposed to be easy as pie, but not the pie she baked nice and mouth-meltin' in her own kitchen for the few customers she was willin' to take on.

By the time she got through paintin' to directions, bottles of 'em, cans of 'em, folders of 'em, the paint was so thick it shriveled up like a fallen souffle, and the honey-dew that was supposed to been cream turned the worst tattle-tale gray that ever hung on Mrs. Bowler's line. And with the damp winds blowin' off Lake Ontario it stayed sticky as a lollipop.

"What we need is a real bookcase — mahogany with glassed-in doors like Mrs. Dreyton's."

"Ceilin's not high enough."

"I don't mean no sectarian. She has a glassed-in bookcase, too."

"And more dough than what we got."

"I notice when it's bad smellin' stuff for yer gentleman's garden, we got enough cash. Well, I want a gentleman's settin' room with learnin' countin' for somethin'—"

"Don't you go buyin' on time, Cora. Pay as you go, I say. Even Truman's comin' round to it."

It took plenty of jawin' plus what was hid in the British lion mug to get Hal to spend fifty dollars and up for a real elegant book-case. The man showed her one of them crescendas with fancy grille work, but it was over a hundred. She settled for a seventy-nine dollar bookcase with the kind of glass doors that slid back like an overhangin' garage door. The mahogany was red-brown like the leather, with a grain that rippled along like music. The books fit in it comfy as a moccasin except for the year book which belonged out on the table, anyhow, lookin' read.

With the Britannica in all the elegance of glass and mahogany, rows straight as the Cold Stream Guards, she worried on account of the shine on the glass hidin' the fine red morocco and the gold letterin'. Still and all, no dust could get to 'em, Hal wasn't as like to lay papers and gardenin' leaflets between the shelves, and no neighbor kid could mark 'em up with chalk. A pity you couldn't put the entire case under glass to keep Dinty from sharpenin' his claws on her one bit o' mahogany.

Whenever she removed the bookcase, strainin' her back and shoulder shovin' it from wall to wall, the furniture seemed to folla it around. Somethin' had to go. It couldn't be Hal's chair or his hassock or his pipe rack, and he wouldn't hear of puttin' the radio in the dinin' room. It had to be her plant stand and sewin' table. Over by the winda, where she'd had the shelves in the first place, was the best she could do. She hung the lace curtains she'd been savin' fer she didn't know what, and bought a ready-made slip cover for the worse greased chair. Them fine shelves even made her slick up a bit her own self, wear better lookin' aprons, set her hair in curlers more of ten nights, plaster as much cream on her face as she did on the book leather. That leather took so much rubbin' and polishin' with special creams and oils that Hal complained it was gettin' to smell like a shoe shinin' parlor.

NOW HER BRITANNICA was ready for a viewin'. She didn't have no friends to speak of in a town of retired farmers what didn't take kindly to factory workers comin' in from Buffalo, and the swells of the town wouldn't never set and eat the pies and cakes she baked for 'em, with the likes of her. Just the same she was goin' to have a real party viewin' with refreshments. She wouldn't let on what they was invited for, only in Meadville you didn't give a party without no reason, and only Dinty had a birthday comin' up. She'd say they was invited to clean up some pies and cakes left over from a big order.

When it come to spottin' the Britannica, every one of her guests was slow as an old cow at the pail. Matty Brooks bumbled her way to the big vase of peonies she'd set atop the bookcase, gettin' a wet snootful of 'em when she oughta know peonies don't smell much. "Our new Britannica," she told Matty.

"Oh, one of Hal's new hybrids. They're a spankin' fine peony all right."

"No — no, the Britannica is an encyclopedia — twenty-four volumes in all, not countin' the year book."

Matty didn't have to jerk at them glass doors. The rest of 'em was pawin' at the books, breakin' down the backs like they was old shoes, crackin' the bindin's, shuttin' 'em careless. They was too ignorant to give books o' learnin' proper respect. "Careful of them bindin's," she said, about to add, "I only have the loan of them," but she couldn't so much as think of them as not all hers. That was what was baked hard into this batter all right, a naggin' doubt about keepin' 'em. Her daughter-in-law could jerk 'em back anytime they got more room.

One afternoon along in November, the light shinin' cold on the glass doors of the bookcase, she felt a bit let down. The viewin' was over, the pastor had paid his respects to 'em, they was housed in the best of bookcases and fed their conditionin' creams and oils, and there they were and there she was, and it was mighty quiet in that settin' room.

She rolled back the glass doors and let her glance warm itself on the red-brown leather. A volume slid out nice and easy, the date set among the golden thistle — 1768 — the Encyclopaedia's founding year, before there ever was a United States of America. She let the pages slip away to the slippery-cool pitchers — the restful grays and darks, colors like a band strikin' up. One title folded into another slick as butter foldin' into a batter. Rhodes-Rhythm-Richelieu-Rimini.

Toward the end of the volume, a pitcher took her for a ride like she was on horse-back or on a burro up them craggy mountains to San Marino. She could almost hear bells ringin' round the mountain, smell air as clear. Trouble was, she stayed in San Marino so long, she was late gettin' Hal's supper on the table.

Afternoons — mornin's even — whenever her work would let her just set, she'd slide out a volume, stirring up a leather smell that took her to far places before she so much as set eyes on a pitcher. Pages fallin' away fast had a smell all their own, the shiny richer'n the plain. She'd take out settin' time she didn't rightly have, feelin' wicked little chills up her spine as she'd rub flour off her hands or dry 'em on her apron, and open another book to its pitchers. It was like the pitchers want you, and when you come to them, you both live.

Time was fit to boil over while she turned to Heraldry, the Thames in fog, a wayside shrine on the ridges of the Andes, a market place in Bou Saada, safes, strong rooms and vaults for children, and children's children, and children's children's children.

The near became part and parcel of the far. Lookin' out at the water tower on the hill; she'd see mosques and minarets; the air blowin' off Lake Ontario, smell of leaves burnin', winter branches, they belonged to every far place. At night, the colors would slip off the shiny pages to dance behind closed lids.

After runnin' back and forth from her bakin' to the books, washin' her hands often as a doc, there come a time when she all but give outa new pitchers; they was gettin' familiar as her afghan. Some she went back and back to on purpose — San Marino, her first love, cloud forms, a Chinese snow scene by an unknown artist, cathedral of Altamura.

From readin' under the pitchers she took to samplin' bits what wasn't. A coupla turns from Abyssinia, her eyes fell on Actaeon, that Diana had killed just for catchin' her in the act of bathin', whoever Diana was.

And Beatrice Cenci — what a time she had back in 1577, locked up in a lonely castle by a father what didn't have no good intentions.

No wonder he was killed in his bed, but that poor Beatrice got beheaded for it.

All mighty interestin', but then there was a lot of double talk like when she wanted to know about the birth of a star and got fouled up with nebulae, shrinkage and equatorial planes to say nothin' of density of the order of 10^{31} grammes per cubic centimeter. Just readin' along not understandin' was a kind of music, all she didn't know, a hunger better'n what you got hangin' over the stove, cookin', and bakin', and talkin' of food.

From readin' what her eyes fell on she took to lookin' up subjects on purpose — London, Royal Doulton pottery, her own Lancashire. Before she knew it, she was lyin' on her stomach on the rug readin' like when she was a kid. The Britannica was sort of a self-help super market where you shopped for subjects, some on your list, some comin' to mind by what you see.

All ways possible she'd make the books hers, yet they wasn't quite. That daughter-in-law could call 'em in anytime. Same thing happened to that high and mighty Mrs. Bufert with her drum and fife dinin' room set. After half a lifetime with the loan of 'em, her sister in Pasadena wanted them back all of a sudden.

Whatever come, with the Britannica under her roof, folks was pesterin' her for more'n pies and cakes, and that even went for the ladies of The Seven Lively Arts club, just about the snootiest gatherin' in town. Her hands was all over dough from the bread she was bakin' the day Mrs. Bufert come to her door mumblin' somethin' about a settin' hen she wanted to look up in the Britannica.

"A settin' hen, Ma'am?" And she couldn't help addin', "I didn't know as how a cock could so much as crow on your side o' town."

"Heavens, not a real hen — a china hen — antique. I'm reading a paper on period china before our club."

Mrs. Bufert sure was an ignoramus around an encylopedia. Cora had to look everything up for her, and when she found the place, all but had to rub her nose in the right paragraphs.

Other ladies of The Seven Lively Arts club had to be shown their way around the Britannica, too. When it come Mrs. Lynton's time to look up her speech, Cora asked her, "Now that I have the Britannica and all, and can make some real good speeches, why don't you make me a member?"

"Well, it isn't just the weekly speeches," said Mrs. Lynton. "What then? I'd throw in the pies and cakes every Wednesday, free of charge."

Mrs. Lynton stood there stiff as new book bindin'. "According to our constitution a member must be — well, a native daughter —"

"Native? Native of what? My ancestors was natives of England long before yours ever saw Meadville. And the Magna Charta givin' us free rights is older'n your constitution."

Mrs. Lynton was hikin' up a nostril like a distress signal, but they wasn't no Seven Lively Arters around. "You'd better vote me in," Cora told her, "or there'll be no more Wednesday bakin's free of charge or other ways, and no Britannica — not a smell."

That oughta do it. She had her first speech all thought out by the time the ladies come again for their cakes. "You folks can look forward to hearin' about Royal Doulton ware when you vote me in," she told Mrs. Bufert and Mrs. Lynton.

"We've already considered your membership at last Wednesday's meeting," said Mrs. Bufert, "and the majority feels that our constitution must stand as it was handed down to us."

Just the same, she wasn't no factory reject. She could talk with the best o' them now, even argue with the pastor over the cradle of civilization. Why should church suppers keep her back in the kitchen while them as thought they could sing and speech-make moved in on the church parlor to perform? When a missionary evenin' was comin' up for their Lucy Ballard on the island of Ceylon, Cora spoke up as how she know'd enough about Ceylon to give a talk.

To keep her knees from knockin' together when her time come, she pretended as how she was just standin' in the kitchin wavin' a spoon and talkin' on to dad about somethin' she'd read. "What was you expectin' outa me," she started in natural like, "a grunt? I got somethin' to say about that island, and it ain't all pretty. Would ya believe it, Ceylon is such a heathen place that there's over three million Buddhists, over a million Hindus, and only five hundred and fifty-five thousand Christians, which puts a lot of work in the lap of Lucy Ballard." They was bustin' right into the middle of her speech with their hand clappin'. Why there was nothin' to this learnin' business — nothin' to it. You just read up on things, and said what ya read.

That speech got over so good she figgered they'd want more.

"How about somethin' on primitive religions?" she asked the head of the program committee. "No," he said like she was in some castin' office. "We're heavily booked for some time to come."

Folks around here just didn't want real learnin', genuine facts, they'd rather have them piddlin' lantern slides, or piana playin', or Miss Naylor's bleatin'. Even folks what come for pies and cakes didn't want to learn nothin' while she boxed 'em. No use tellin' 'em that it takes four thousand three hundred pounds of paint to cover the Capitol dome, or that the sparkle in champagne is due to imperfect fermentation.

Anyhow she got back into the way of just dreamin' over the pitchers, lettin' her eye catch sentences here and there. Them were the best Britannica days before she got to showin' off her learnin' like a new fur coat.

Just when she found her way back to the books for simon-pure love of 'em, her son wrote he was movin' into a new apartment. He didn't say nothin' about the books, but she couldn't stand not knowin'. She phoned him long distance .... "I'm prepared to send 'em back," she said, trying not to talk too loud into the phone .... "Send back what, mother?" the boy asked .... "The Britannica, I know it was only a loan." "What brought that on? We didn't ask for it, did we?"

Her daughter-in-law got on the wire. "Are they in your way, Mother Burridge?" "Oh no, but I thought now you was in a new apartment —" ... "We're higher up," said her son, "but we have less room —"

"I can't stand this not knowin'," Cora said, "either take 'em back or give 'em outright." Her daughter-in-law was back on the wire. "I'd like to think we could count on them some day when we might have a house with a library" ... "When that time comes," her son put in, "we'll be wanting a new edition. Keep them — they're yours."

"You mean you give 'em to me outright?"

"Yes, mother, outright."

The Britannica was all hers. She walked over to the shelves feelin' free — free of a loan, of chasin' after fancy clubs with 'em, speechifyin', showin' 'em off as six hundred dollars worth of learnin'.

Settin' time or no, they was hers to come to — pitchers wantin' her, springin' to life under her eyes — mountains of the earth and mountains of the moon, spiral nebulae and protozoa — the world from Al at Lloyd's to Zygote.

[Carolina Quarterly]

ALWAYS GOOD FOR A BELLY LAUGH

THE MAN WAS A CIRCUS on blades, his solemn tussles with the ice good for a belly laugh at every flop. Night after night, skaters going round and round Rockefeller rink left off to watch; people jammed the red rail, threw a cordon of laughter around the Plaza above; diners in the French and English grilles on either side of the rink were convulsed behind plate glass.

"Must be a funny man from some ice show," the onlookers speculated. ... "Hired by the rink perhaps." ... "Looks like an undertaker in that dark homburg." The skaters pieced together what they could learn of him .... "Harvard graduate" ... "Statistician with some brokerage house in Wall Street" ... "Commutes from Montclair."

The formality of this bone of a man in Brooks Brothers clothing, his air of having just emerged from a board meeting to pay his respects to the ice, that was the architecture for his comic fall. He was anyone in authority you'd want to pull the rug out from under, but before you got there he pulled out his own rug in a fight for balance that laid him low.

In a bit of business with tight-wrapped umbrella and bulging briefcase, he would come out on the ice with a carriage so erect that he all but leaned over backwards, a fall from his eminence unthinkable. Or he would clap a Tyrolean hat on his head, and consult endlessly unfolding time tables and road maps before mounting an imaginary bike and plunging toward the plate glass of the English grille.

Whenever he rested by the rail, his precise features in repose verging on good looks, most skaters by-passed him as if their laughter had thrown up a barbed-wire entanglement between them. In the skatehouse they acted embarrassed to see him sitting there packed tight in his reserve.

Travers knew his effect on the other skaters; he had felt that way himself when he went back to the theater for something he'd forgotten, and an unshaded light was a cold eye on the empty stage.

The laugh was on him two seasons ago when all this started, not controlled by him, but on him. He had come down to the rink with his wife and two boys. Harriette had refused to change from her lacy pumps into rented skates with their green-painted heels. "You'll never catch me making a fool of myself out on that ice," she'd said, "for the whole world to see."

When he was thirteen he could have skated dizzying circles around both his boys, but out there on the ice for the first time in twenty-five years, he could scarcely keep his feet. His long habit of carrying himself straight as a flagpole threw him ludicrously off balance, as he could see by the mirrored columns in the grille, and hear by the laughter all around. The old balance came back to him fast enough, the knee bend instead of the swing from the hips, but he still played the beginner just for laughs, that red rail like a little red schoolhouse where he studied the comedian's art.

As blade and ice fused in a power that sent him in a glissando across the rink to roars of laughter at his pretzel-like knotting by the rail, he felt the power of that great gold Prometheus up there above the fountain, his gift to mortals not mere fire for their cook stoves but the fire of laughter.

Back by the skate-house Harriette had covered her disgusted little nose with her veil. His boys weren't laughing either, not even nine-year-old Brock. In his own childhood he might not have been as clever as some others, but he knew the give-and-take of laughter. He'd do anything to get laughs — mimic, grimace, let himself in for bad marks by muffing translation, making such ridiculous mistakes that even his teachers had to laugh.

What he'd do for a laugh all but prostrated an Averill family, accustomed to laughs as discreet as their coughs whenever they couldn't avoid seeing the joke. Averills never clowned; they sat on the bench, ran for office, founded colleges, but they never clowned.

"We're not amused," his mother would say at his groping humor, and when his father died, he and his younger brother were locked in such a struggle to be first with their mother, her idea of head of the family, that he turned into quite a somber young man.

As for girls, if you wanted them you couldn't be both clown and lover, catching them up in your arms while you sprawled at their feet. Besides, the Averill in him was not amused. He had no use for funny men either, regarded them as low life. Broad humor was something to discard along with growing pains even if it left him without anything in which he excelled. He had started out a whiz at track until the doctor said his heart couldn't take extraordinary strain. "Nature has compensated for a slight valvular lesion, but if you don't favor your heart a bit, compensation will no longer work for you."

Tonight he felt the soaring power of his skill as the laughter from above fell in leis about him. Almost three seasons now, he'd worn them — his alone ever since he'd slipped back without Harriette and the boys to try out his clowning.

In high silk hat and his grandfather's silver-headed cane, he was dancing around in gingerly rhythm, stiff as a ruler about to take the measure of the ice, when his mother and sister came down to the rail. He wouldn't stop off yet, not while the laughter of the crowd was feting him. No one from his other life had any business thrusting in here, making him feel it was a vice to get laughs, like hitting the bottle or taking up with some woman when you had a perfectly good home.

Snow crystals cut by the blades of many skaters tingled like the laughter. He felt power, felt smoothness, felt rhythm beneath his blades. His mother and sister standing there as if they were no part of him, he'd make them laugh, rip it out of them. In every fall from his height it was his family who fell, generations of pride going down with him his younger brother's plaster pomp went crashing while he, Travers, rose — rose to his skill, his comedian's art.

Hanging onto his silk topper and holding fast to his grandfather's cane, he began to fold, give way, melt into the ice, laughter wrapping him round like warm quilting. As he went through the droll business of righting himself without loss of hat or cane, he glanced across to his mother and sister. They were frozen at the rail. The crowd was with him, their laughter the streamers drawing him around in carnival mood before he could catch his breath. Here he was king — those two would have to wait for their audience.

Harriette might as well be frozen at the rail along with them. Since their marriage she had become more one with his family than with him. Her sense of fitness was tight as her bra; you couldn't shake up laughs. When Harriette — never to be addressed as Hat or Hatty — had been one of the battery of stenographers in his uncle's brokerage house, her eyes looking up at him had been blue fields of adoration. She was his short stuff, a nestling kitten like the one he had sneaked home in a big paper bag — all his, if his mother would let him keep a stray.

Like the kitten, she turned out to be more the family's than his, often looking past him to his brother as head of the family, copied his mother and sister with alarming results, a little thing trying to dress tall and talk overbearing, catching up their mannerisms faster than their manners, and affixing her own funny idea of fitness. She made delicious errors in her reach for big words, her rule-book parties. It was fun to guide her tastes as that anxious-to-please little frown drew her tendril-like brows together. She had a morning face, so fresh and pink it needed very little done to it, her hair, fine-skeined. He had never let her alter her child's bob to one of his sister's striking coifs. Oh, he loved her all right — it would never be another woman — just this, this ice fever.

The last time Harriette or the boys had ever come down to the rail, he had perfected his routine enough to want them to see his act, to let go a little, then a little more until they were laughing with the others. As pre-schoolers their laughter romped all around his antics, but exposed to Harriette and his own family, they winced at loss of dignity, especially in their father. That night, only his youngest had let out a belly laugh — hastily sucked in — at his solemn contemplation of a small globe of the world in his hand while his skates were about to slide out from under him.

Whether his family laughed or not, when the flags of all nations, took the gusts of the Plaza as if whipped by the laughter going around, it was life itself to be out there on the ice. All thought of Harriette and the boys glanced off his blades, went swirling away with the snow crystals that stung his face like a flying theater curtain. On blades, the oldest laugh routines were new as if you were the first comic who ever flopped for a belly laugh.

Back by the rail his wife and mother were inclining their heads, yet lowering them in a way that told him they were overhearing chatter about him. "Bones," he'd overhead himself called. "Bones" ... "Bonesey" ... a nickname he hadn't heard since his clowning school-days.

A long line of Averills skated around with him, and whenever he fell, they all sprawled. If he'd kept his dignity, his name on the door might be up with the members of the firm, one day, instead of at the lower left, but his legs were too long and restless to be wedged in at a statistician's desk; he could only wander from it when the ice waited for him, neat as a poker chip, smooth as a watch crystal.

The instant he lost his job, his brother spread a landing net, ready to take him into his firm. "In those brother teams," he'd heard said often enough, "one is usually the brains, has to carry the weight." He wasn't going to be the lesser brother.

With the first cut of his blade, this new season, Harriette, who always looked to him for decisions, made one of her own. "I'm not going on like this. Your brother will arrange a divorce — see that the boys are looked after." Not a lone decision then, his brother had helped her along with it.

When he saw that she meant what she said about the divorce, he stayed away from the ice, looked for a job so fast that he fancied himself on skates along the smooth marble corridors, gliding from frosted door to frosted door; even practiced a spin while waiting for the elevator.

Harriette — he couldn't imagine any kind of life without his short stuff, her hair in its child's bob, soft as a kitten to the touch. And the boys, he wanted to be with them constantly throughout their growing years; he wanted them to be his sons. Just the same it was no good making him choose — not yet. He could only try to hang onto both, like the hat and cane that sent him headlong to the ice.

Forced evenings at home wrapped all the disconsolate times when skating sessions were called off because the sun had melted away the ice or the rain was beating down on it. Everything about the house was static, waiting — the smoothed bed-spread, the crystal centerpiece, Harriette's fingers on the glassine cover of a rented book. In a cell where he could neither stand nor sit nor breathe, all of him was out there soaring across the ice.

Night after night he would close his eyes to such a reeling head that he was no longer lying motionless; he was some sort of toreador who had slain boredom, and was being borne up on the laughing shoulders of the crowd. On his job interview, next morning, he would act fuzzy, played out, a bad forty risk.

The ice he wore lightly as a charm on his watch chain — his jewel, his diamond, the perfect circle. Fast ice, slow ice, it was all his, the fast ice of April, a mirror lake for a swan-like glide ending in a fall that left him wringing out his trouser cuffs; slow ice, hard, resistant, his blades scrabbling for a foothold as he skated under the giant Christmas tree when he should have been home decorating his own. Whatever the season he always skated away with the laughs. After all the reticent years, it was good to be out there making an unholy show of himself.

Each time the men cleared the ice between sessions, obliterating the skaters' marks, a bit of himself was obliterated. Summer could only be a fretful waiting. He would stand looking down on what used to be his watch-crystal ice, now mushrooming with umbrella'd tables, Muzak still playing its skating rhythms, attendants turning the hose on boxed trees and plants instead of ice for the session.

One indoor rink stayed open in the summer, but only a few unsmiling skaters went around in the damp mausoleum air, condensation from the ceiling dropping on them like cold sweat. Seeing himself in the fearsome expanse of mirror, he was so lean and sorry-looking that he wondered why anyone ever laughed.

"Travers — Travers — here." His sister cast off her usual come-to me attitude through a slightly unbalancing lean over the red rail, but in an elegant reach of her leopard sleeve, she tried to rake him in with a croupier's gesture. He could have felt close to Roz if she'd let him. She was something of a comic jack-in-the-box, too, the lid secured except for an occasional rusty-springed quip.

In a running slide across the ice he lurched to the rail where his mother and sister stood, doffed his silk topper and fell flat to laughter they gathered their furs against. That might be a creeper of a smile across Roz's face except that she always had the look of smiling her disdain. One smile from Roz would mean more than the roars of all the rest. As children, when he had the schoolyard in laughter, Roz would just walk away.

No, he'd spare them nothing; he'd go through desperate attempts to right himself, and flop again, and again, bringing their pride down with him.

"Get up — will you get up?" said Roz.

He just squatted there at her feet, partly to catch his breath. That shortness of breath was getting more bothersome, and the swelling in his ankles made them feel ready to burst his laces.

"This is the only place we can find you, these days," said his mother.

"We have something urgent to discuss."

"Won't you step into my office?" he panted, doffing his topper again. His mother had a way of looking past him, her profile the only part of her face he ever called up. The fullness of her gaze had always belonged to his brother. "Don't you think so, Brock?" she'd say. "What's your opinion, Brock?" Brock couldn't help her now, as she stood there in the conservative sealskins worn by generations of Averill women.

Roz looked past everyone, past him now to remark, "Mighty short of breath, aren't you? And your color — it's blue. Your heart's not up to your clowning."

In the mirror column beyond, he could see that his skin had a faintly bluish cast like the remains of clown's paint. "Reasonable exercise, yes, your heart has compensated to that extent," she was going on, "but not, uh — this unholy show."

Harriette had gone through the same thing with him, adding sobs to her sound effects. "It's not just the fool you're making of yourself, the career you're tossing away — my having lost you — it's what all this may do to your heart." Poor short stuff, she'd only miss what little there was of his brother in him.

The crowd above was clapping for him ... "Hey, Topper, do your stuff." ... "Get going, High-hat." ... "Shake a blade." ...

"Why, that rabble is actually calling for you," said his mother, "as if you were some sort of paid entertainer."

"Let's go into the English grille," said Roz, "where we can be semi-private."

Pell-mell off the points of his skates he headed for the plate glass of the grille, glumly inspected the diners, making a pretzel of himself to scan a menu in someone's hand, pulled out empty pockets, tipped an apologetic hat, and slunk back to his mother and sister, turning the spotlight of laughter on them.

"Travers, listen to me," said his mother. "It's not too late even now. Harriette says she'll call off divorce proceedings if she has any assurance you'll stop playing the clown."

"A good way to convince her is to land a job," said Roz. "I've just heard of an opening. No, your brother has nothing to do with this. Just get in touch with a Mr. Donaldson of Donaldson and Struthers, 51 Pine Street."

Travers did a back flip away from them — out to a nice round belly of a rink — a belly full of laughter.

In a leap that powered his blades, he took a sudden turn off the ice to the skate-house. As he opened his locker, Roz came to the doorway. "Leaving?" she asked.

He was too short of breath to do anything but shake his head, No.

By the time he'd exchanged his topper for a homburg, his cane for a *Wall Street Journal*, Roz was gone from the doorway.

Coming out on the ice, he saw that his mother and sister had moved to a more inconspicuous curve of the rail. He unfurled his *Wall Street Journal* and dallied about on the ice so absorbed in stock quotations that he tripped, righted himself, tripped again. That should blast laughter out of those two. He looked across the ice. They weren't at the rail, or by the skate-house, or in the English grille; they weren't anywhere.

The rink was all his again. Later, he might regret this — the finality of their leaving, what they'd say to Harriette — later — now his blades were too swift for awareness of anything but the ice — all thought of the boys lost in the laughter that ringed him round. He had the crowd on the point of his blade. The season was only just beginning — he'd have a long run. This was his glittering stage, and the stars above were bits of smooth, fast ice, a million rinks awaiting his blades; and he'd skate from star to star along a milky way of laughter.

PEOPLE in the Plaza above pushed and jostled for a better look at the funny man's new routine, laughed their insides out at his solemn business with the newspaper, his pencil worrying at the margin. Then the rarest yet — a regular dying swan, a droll collapse, his homberg rolling off. Usually so careful of his props, he let the newspaper get away from him, sheets flying high as a kite, tangling around the legs of skaters as guards went on frantic chase. His impeccable timing was off, too; he stayed down too long in a tedious gasp for breath. They began to clap for him, the steady clap, clap, clap of a movie audience for a broken film to be spliced.

A waltzing couple skated over with his crushed homberg, bent over him as if in real concern, motioned for the guards. They helped him up, his legs weak as macaroni. This was no act — this was on the level. Of course he could be faking a collapse at the stock-market news, but the guards didn't think so. They brought him into the skate-house, and laid him on a bench out of sight of the other skaters.

The crowd waited a long time for his reappearance, but he didn't come back on the ice that night. Those who waited above the skate-house saw the two men help him carefully up the stairs, his face a deathly blue.

"Heart attack," the manager said. "We brought him around." "You won't see that bird on the ice again," said one of the skaters. "I don't know," said his partner, tightening her laces. "I don't know. I think he's a chronic like us, and when you're a chronic, there's no place else."

The rink settled to its round of skaters throughout a winter so cold that few but the regulars came out on the ice, and almost no spectators stood in the down-drafts from the great buildings above. It was no place to go for laughs anymore. Without their funny man, the skaters looked like a bunch of bedraggled stooges.

Along in April when the tulips by the Prometheus fountain were bobbing stiffly as beginners on their blades, he came out on the ice one Sunday evening in the striped trousers and cutaway he must have had on that morning as church usher, convulsed them with a best-man-at-the-wedding routine. He marched cautiously up the aisle, shaking imaginary rice from his handkerchief, fumbling through his pockets for the ring.

His blades gliding faster and faster, he caught up with a skater in white, and just as he was about to kiss the bride, pretzeled down at her feet, untwisted himself, knotted, flopped — the laughs all his.

[Originally published in *Prairie Schooner*,
and selected for *Best American Short Stories*, 1952]

MONEY BOY

THROUGH A GLASS PANE to the darkened ballroom Ralph could see his son along a runway that was like a golden bar in suspension, white-lighting the boy's hair, minting his features to coin-like perfection.

In his eleven years Peter had paraded down miles of runway ... four years old when Helen had asked, "What possible harm to let him model? With you just out of the army-unsettled — well, we could use that ten dollars an hour." His "I don't know, I just don't know, I need time to think things through," twisted down her mouth to something like a scar. "Think things through, think things through. You spend so much time thinking things through that you're no nearer a job than you were months ago — idea man, merchandising brain — no plan ever shined up enough to submit."

Still thinking things through while his son paraded the runway with all the self possession of six years experience and seven thousand a year average income, paraded in the angel-smile knowledge that no modeling agency could handle all his business — his own wire, own set of account books, bills printed with his professional name, Barry Brooks. His father's name wouldn't do, not Wortman, plain Peter Wortman.

Someone behind the scenes had laid on Peter's suntan make-up with a heavy hand. Too earthen for his smile, the stuff clogging his pores, not letting them breathe, like the golden boy he had read about, dancer at some pagan feast, his skin painted gold from head to toe, sealed against all natural function until he had died in his dance.

In the flash of camera bulbs blinded tots, warned back by ballroom attendants, stopped short above the dark chasm, the drop to nothingness at the end of their lighted course. "While it lasts," Helen would say, "just while it lasts," crowding his schedule almost beyond the possible in dread that such radiance would no more stay with him than a choir boy's voice. Lately the boy even outdid his mother raking his hours for all the money in them. The plan at the start was to build a bank account not to be touched except for his education, and then they began dipping into it to live — live better — his junior-high sister wanting more and more. The money would be returned as soon as he came up with a sound merchandising idea, but how-could he in the midst of this razzle dazzle? After all, he was the boy's manager, a business in itself if Helen would let him conduct it properly instead of snarling up every problem trying to solve it herself, and dribbling away his time with errands and details.

Forty a week jobs were kicking around, the kind he had held in Wanamaker's Adjustment Department before the war, but Helen would twist her mouth down at a weekly pittance in the light of her son's earnings. Only big money could begin to restore the boy's bank account and his own self esteem.

All the youngsters were being hustled down the runway in a grand finale of back-to-school fashions. Tots guided by the older models tried to look past their light into a darkness thorned with laughter at their confusion. Entire families at work — twins, toddler sister, small brother in red-faced protest against the twins' efforts to open his bathrobe and show his pajamas.

Peter and a little girl slick as pottery glaze strolled along-in brother-and-sister ski suits, their smiles set for the flash, hers a show of teeth, his curving around his long upper lip. The boy seldom bothered to display his teeth, no need to break out in any such dazzlement when an easy smile would do. The back-to-school clothes Peter was modeling in May, he'd get wholesale by September to parade on perpetual runway before his classmates, contemptuously discarding clothes worn only a few times, his money on parade, too, in lavish treats, charge accounts that Helen let him run up beyond all reason.

Whenever he tried to discipline the boy, Helen would make a move toward her precious bar of gold. "Not now, Ralph. Not now. Don't upset him, he has an important call tomorrow," or "He can't stand a scene. He's had a hard day."

Hard day today, big day tomorrow, looks not to be disturbed — no such outs this time. Nothing could hold off a showdown over the eight hundred and sixty dollar binge he'd just been on, a show-down they should have had the night the runaway was brought home, fashion parade or no. He must be called to account, not so much for what he'd just done as for character lapses all along the line. *Whose? Peter's or yours?* The question jolted into his mind with the medicinal tones of his own father calling him to account over the jars and bottles of the apothecary shop he could never get his father to modernize. Couldn't pass an old-time apothecary shop today without wanting to smash it. Sometimes he would stare into the liquid amber globe like the amber rays in his son's grey eyes, wanting to be the companion to his son that his father never was to him.

Sports together never worked with Helen shrilling like a macaw over seven-thousand-dollar-a-year skin burned, peeled, darkened; eyes blackened in ball games; bones broken on skis, ice skates. The boy, himself, wasn't much interested except for late afternoon swimming and indoor fencing as possible beauty builders. Would do him good to break his noble damn nose, flatten nostrils that sneered slightly at his father along with his tease, his taunt of a smile, his *wouldn't you like to be in my golden sandals?*

Ralph went behind the scenes as the children stepped off the runway, their smiles gone with the flash bulbs. Mothers hurrying to the ladies room with whimpering tots, detoured one little fellow screaming out a temper tantrum on the ballroom floor.

Hidden by screens, the older models were changing into their clothes. Change, change, change, that's all the boy ever did — changing from one costume to another uncomfortable fashion months ahead of season — bathing suits in January, ski suits in May. This afternoon, at least, he could wear winter mufflers and ski boots in an air-conditioned ballroom instead of one of those airless photographic studios where the photographers cussed the heat in their shirt sleeves while Peter stood for endless retakes in fleece-lined jackets and fur-trimmed hoods. Maybe character was wanting in many ways, but he had a certain kind of guts, his grandfather's kind, keeping his drugstore open as long as there was money to take in, standing in the hard light of his globes, his fool's moustache as walrus-backward as his drugstore, treating Ralph like some dolt of an employee, saying *No* to his ideas before he could get them out.

Son, mother, stood before the mirror column, the boy all-souled in renewing the part in his white gold hair, his mother smoothing his jacket across his shoulders as if she were girding him in valiant armor. Her hair, once his, was now dyed in brassy remembrance, all her laid-away longings unfolding again in him. She was always worrying for fear his hair would darken, sifting it for gold a thousand times a day. Her mind had always been on every golden stirring, first in the crib beside their bed, then the little bed by theirs. Now she listened for sounds on the other side of the wall. She would interrupt their most intimate moments to catch the least sound in the night. He wasn't much of a lover, he supposed; had tried to mean more to her, but that boy wouldn't let him — just by *being*, he wouldn't let him.

Lost in his own image until Ralph intercepted it with an incautious wave of his hat, Peter left off looking at himself to appraise his father along the doubtful press of his suit to the wrong break in his trouser leg which his son informed him came of not wearing suspenders.

"If the car's parked to hell and gone, drive it around, will you?" said Peter, his tone a silken order. "After four hours on parade I don't feel like much of a trek."

"Eighth Avenue and Fifty-fourth was the best I could do during rush hour."

"Retake," said Peter. "We'll stay down for dinner and a show."

"But your sister," said Helen, touching away the shadow of a frown from between his brows, "she's expecting us home, and Myrtle's working overtime to cook you a roast — pan browned potatoes the way you like them — strawberry shortcake. I thought that's what you wanted, a good dinner, and then television."

"You said yourself that television isn't good for my eyes. That's when I have real frown lines."

Books gave him frown lines, too — the books he brought home to him, unread. Helen was always reminding him to save those amber-rayed eyes, the grey of his father's and the brown of his mother's touched to light. Reading aloud to him was no good to him either, nor any talk or discussion beyond his peacock world, the slick appeal of manners, dress, money.

"Just phone home, Helen," said Peter. "Tell them we've changed our plans — we're staying down. They're used to it by this time."

"But I'm not," said Ralph.

Peter looked at him curiously, as if a pet goldfish had almost said something through the glass ... Peter, the man of the house in his mother's eyes. She dressed to please him, revolved the family schedule around his job needs, set the table to his whims, getting him to eat what he should only on pleas that one dish would benefit his teeth, another his hair, another his complexion. She bulged scrapbook after scrapbook with his photos and write-ups; papered an alcove with a nauseous photomontage of his poses from five on through.

"No show tonight, son, not with all I have to say to you."

"It's kept this long. Why not longer?" said Peter as he went on ahead, scattering smiles like so many free samples. His son was becoming every glad-handing business man Ralph had ever despised, ingratiating himself with those who could do him the most good. Despise? Was that it? Or did he envy? What kind of a smile could he manage with that thin-rolling upper lip? No more than his own father with his buckram mouth; he must have been unsure of himself behind those jars and bottles, before his five sons at table, not with him so much, he was never the mother's favorite. But Peter — Peter was sure as the sun.

"Now that the fashion parade is over you can afford to disarrange your features a bit over your conduct this last —"

"Not now," said Helen. "The boy has been on his feet since one o'clock this afternoon."

"There's the place to have dinner," said Peter as they passed the Opal Room. "Jimmy Durante in person."

Taking hold of Peter's arm, Ralph marched him by the Opal Room. "That place would cost a young fortune," he told him.

"Well, I make a young fortune," said Peter. "I earn my fun."

Down the length of the lobby and out into the street they had to cut a swath through wondering stares at the boy. Alongside his sure-walking son, he felt conscious of his own defects, his inturning ankle since a foot injury at basketball practice, his eyes deep and near set like misers in their caves, the deadness of his skin beside the boy's.

"Turn off that flash-bulb smile, can't you?" he told Peter. "You're on your own time now."

If they could develop some talent in him except for showing his face. Helen had tried to interest him in dramatics. "Even in modeling you have to act," she had told him. "Models with half your looks pile up engagements because they can act out their scenes." Striving was no part of Peter's nature. Like a beautiful girl he was content in just being. "You'll look foolish later on," Ralph had told him, "when you're balding and can't do a damn thing."

No use trying to put color in the boy's wan fancies — metal working, rock formation — no use sending him to a private school, sweating to pull his marks up to passing grades, when the boy's smile knew that sometimes — sometimes he'd give his soul to be his own son.

"That's the world's best steak house," said Peter, trying to slow down as they neared the parked car. "You know you could go for a sirloin right now, Ralph — baked potatoes with chive butter." Angel's own smile of having his will — his way. Not tonight he wouldn't.

"Don't call me Ralph. How many times must I tell you to say Dad?"

"Why, it's charming," said Helen, trying to high heel along on her broad arches. "Everyone says it's charming."

Their yellow convertible was wedged in almost bumper to bumper-the boy's idea of a car, not his. He took out the keys to their neat jingle, one item his son didn't possess. The boy had to steal his way to the car last spring, his smile not quite so easy when a police officer picked him up on the parkway.

Peter relaxed control of his posture the instant his weary spine hit the green leather upholstery. He closed his eyes to the touch of his mother's hand smoothing hair that some photographers ruffled the way they would disarrange a model room to make it look more lived in.

"Going home is a good idea after all, Dad," he said, his tones nestling up to him. The boy and he were of a piece in not wanting the effort of anger.

"Tonight, home doesn't mean strawberry shortcake and TV. We're going to have things out. What you've done is more serious than you —" No amount of wrenching at the wheel would budge the car. He had to back into the bumpers of the rear car to get free of the curb.

"Parkway," said Peter. "I want to see the ships."

"You know it's jammed at this hour."

"That's the least you can do," said Helen, "after the hard day's work the boy has put in for us."

"Please him no matter what he does. Is that the way to build character? Your clatter wins anyway. You've made me miss the turn."

The *Caronia* was at the pier, her sea green illusion drabbing the waters of the Hudson. "Sweetest ship afloat," said Peter, all but standing, his hair a banner of light above the yellow paint of the roadster. "I'll stake the family to a cruise, this summer."

"You've just had rather an expensive trip."

"Not now," said Helen, "let's not go into it now."

"Not now, always not now. Not now, you'll upset his digestion, not now, you'll interfere with his beauty sleep. He's either resting up for a job or from it. Ruin his character but don't disturb his features. If he steals, don't mention it. Let him go through my wallet, take eight hundred and sixty dollars, and run off to Atlantic City—"

"Hardly stealing, when it's my own money."

"The boy's right," said Helen. "He can't steal what he earns."

The way they lived, wrong was right in shading illusive as the *Caronia*'s ... the man-boy acting on his own before his character was ready for grownup decisions, a character Ralph had wanted to shape to the noble lines of the boy's face. Whenever he wanted Peter to go to church with him, Helen would say, "He needs his rest." It was a rare Sunday that he could walk down the church aisle with his spectacular son, a little embarrassed to have caged the golden bird, yearning after him as Peter sat there beside him, yearning after his future, that is — all he wanted him to be, wanted to be in him.

"Cripes, Dad, you think I helped myself to my own money and went off to Atlantic City because I had to let off steam, go on a binge, like the day I took off for Bear Mountain. Not this time — this time, it was something of a business trip."

Rage against the cool talking boy went into blasts of the horn after a car that cut in too short. A perfect being, set apart, Peter could afford to look serenely photogenic while everyone else purpled. Maybe he didn't have his son's looks, but he had the same desire to stay unruffled.

"As I see it," said Peter, "you're a swell Dad, but business and family just don't mix. I thought in Atlantic City where they have all those beauty contests, maybe I'd find a business manager who'd — well, you know — only take a certain percentage. Then maybe I could have my own bank account and write my own checks, even save enough so I won't have to work when I grow up."

Ralph slammed on the brakes so hard that the car behind sounded an outraged horn. "Why, Ralph, what possessed you? You almost sent the boy against the windshield. You could scar him for life."

The boy's grey eyes were fixed serenely ahead, innocent of all anger as he regarded the curve of the George Washington bridge in a hyacinth haze. Always saving his looks, encasing them in a beauty mask, a mud pack of sweetness. He'd grow old with no more wrinkles than a woman who saves her face-age, puffy under yellowed grey eyes, lean along the jaw, folded into vertical chins.

"You forget, Ralph, you can't treat me like a kid who's not used to long pants. I'm the one who earns for this family. I'm the money boy."

Right when he should tower in his wrath, he had a sense of being in the presence of his father, squirming over nickels and dimes, a short cash register, sense of being physically dwarfed before the son as before the father.

The boy's attention was wandering to the small craft rocking to ropes of light at their buoys by the yacht club. "When do I get a sail-boat like the one just off the bow of the cabin cruiser?"

"You don't make that kind of money, or anywhere near what you think you do."

"Only the kind of money that gets the family a car and a television set and —"

"No more — not one word more. If letting you pose for a few pictures and lord it at an occasional fashion show is doing this to you, then it's time I took over. You'll see what it's like to live on what I can earn." Like any obsolete weapon that might be loaded, his words caused Peter and Helen to look faintly chary. "I mean it. You've tried me too far, this time. Things are going to be different around here. No more modeling for you." Snarl-tongued around his own son as if called on to match his perfection of feature with words that could only fall away before the boy's unreachable smile.

Peter began to yawn with charming insolence, settling to the cushions, his sleepy grey eyes on the forsythia bushes that blonded the parkway. Jerk him to attention, shake his head from his neck like something rotten. That damn tune from a Danny Kaye musical kept taunting through his brain, "Popo the puppet can do anything, do anything, swing on a swing, as long as somebody is pulling his strings." This Popo was cutting his. Tonight he'd work out some merchandising ideas that would reach the desks of top executives. As for an immediate job, he would send letters to every big department store in the city, raise the boy's teasing brows at what his father could do ... *Popo the puppet can do anything, do anything ....*

No more words — they were vague little pings, feeble castings from his worry over the boy's character. He glanced across at Peter only to find that in return to the dignity of silence his son had already preceded him.

By the time they reached home, the silence was getting rather stiff at the joints. Throughout dinner, Helen was in a froth for fear the unsaid might disturb her Peter's digestion even more than words.

WHEN MYRTLE brought on Peter's strawberry shortcake, Ralph excused himself to hunt for his notes in a desk packed tight with Peter's business. They turned up thinner than he remembered, poorly thought out, somewhat dated. In his mind they had grown like a laid-away trophy cup.

Million dollar ideas didn't kick around at the back of desk drawers. He must think — think — but he hadn't been following merchandising trends. Ought to study the trade magazines, go through a few department stores, shop the salesmen, get new ideas that way, not just sit there at his desk like a lobsterman before an empty trap.

Helen came in to darken the room for television. "Can't you think just as well in some other room?" she asked.

"Think — how can a man think in this pleasure-mad family? All anyone can do is manage Peter's small affairs — revolve around Peter — Peter — Peter."

Pocketing his notes and clamping the lid on the portable he had given Peter for his birthday, he made for his room. Better start in by sending out a few letters to the big stores. Peter would hear the typewriter saying things were going to be different around here; he'd hear it talk. *Popo the puppet can do anything, do anything, swing on a swing ....*

Hunt one, peck one, think two, that's how it was when you tried to compose a letter direct to the machine. He'd scrawl the first draft. But what was the good of asking for a job like a hand-out? That wouldn't get him much further than section manager. He was no penny-ante job hunter; he was an idea man. Ideas whizzed you past the outer office to the man at the top desk; slid you in at a top desk of your own. Ideas put men like Bruce Barton and Beardsley Ruml where they were.

Ralph went through his notes again, underscoring any fragments that could be worked into something big. Yawns came up out of nowhere like a lot of crows after seed. *Popo the puppet can do anything, do anything ....*

His father might as well be at his elbow, saying *No* to everything, not letting him get his ideas out. Still he kept at his notes until Helen came in to find him working, and Peter looked in curiously on his way to bed, looked in from the shadow of the hallway to his father in the light.

"You'd better work in the living room," said Helen. "The rest of us have to be up early, you know."

"Go ahead — turn out the light. I think better in the dark," he told her, placing pad and pencil on his desk-table. Ideas would come to him in the electric dark. His best ideas always came with a beat of wings in the night.

"If we're out of here before you're awake," said Helen from her pillow, "remember to pick us up at Hi-Mode, 570 Eighth Avenue at four-thirty tomorrow."

"I know — I know. You've yackity-yacked it a thousand times. Right now I have more important things to think about."

Only *he* had being in the petaled dark that would unfold to ideas ... ideas that could get him through to such merchandisers as Marvin Taplin, Leroy Weiss. All that flashed when he lay back were a bunch of fireflies behind tight-pressed lids. Couldn't shake ideas off some tree of the dark without knowing more about inside workings —plans, policies — plans and policies and plans and ... sleep clouding over, always clouding over before he could reach ideas out of nowhere ... Mustn't let it ... mustn't ...

The heavens wouldn't fall if he didn't shake that tree tonight.
But the boy's character ... a trust, God's trust ... Wanted to shape his
character to the noble lines of his face ... shape his character, shape
his character to the lines, the noble lines ...noble lines ... noble lines
Sleep rocking his bed like a cradle velvety dark-rich sleep dark
cream, luscious dark cream Peter's smile, angel raiment before him,
wings folding him, folding him to rest in him ... father in the son
... son in the father ... father, the son ... son the father ...

[Epoch, Summer 1952]

THE BEST

T HE COLD TINGLED like her good spirits tattooing this bright day into her skin for keeps. She loosened the drawstring of her cary-all for a quick look inside. The best was in there — the best there is.

Best didn't mean Ma's kind no more, not twenty-five cents worth o' the best. Ma used to send her down to Paddys saloon fer it. That was goin' on fifty years ago when she was ten or eleven. They was livin' in Hell's Kitchen over on Forty-sixth street and Tenth avenue so near the docks she could feel the whistles of them big liners right in her chest bones.

Pa worked on the docks when he wasn't took with the weakness. Her Ma had it, too, only more elegant. Pa and Timmy could be scrappin' in the hall, baby Rose fixin' to cry, her big sister, Mildred tryin' to do everything at once, but Ma's be in the parlor layin' on the horse-hair sofa like one o' them ladies of leisure, layin' so's to make the least of a cast in her eye and the most of a figger fine as the rose-painted globe on the erl lamp behind her, a figger she always said she could've taken out of Hell's Kitchen if she hadn't run into Pop.

Outa her wrapper would come a purse and the raw metal shinin' through the silk. "Twenty-five cents worth o' the best," Ma'd say like she was buyin' Brooklyn Bridge.

Tingles of pride would go through her at the Hennesseys takin' nothin' but the best. Their parlor was so full of cherce things that it weren't never used for sleepin'. Ma wouldn't let 'em get near the what-not for so much as a look at the china angels, and doll's tea set, and blue glass hat; and that piano nobody could play, Ma was always shinin' it 'stead o' their shoes.

When Ma said, "Get goin'" the bottle that was to hold the best would be ready wrapped in its blanket of newspapers and snuggle into the big market basket, but it weren't no fish in there, she'd tell the kinds on the block. Just let that fresh Rose Mary Macmenamin dast say she looled like a bundle of old rags with an angle-worm for a mouth, she wouldn't bother to pull her hair out by no roots, she'd sail right on past with her basket, headin' for Paddy's family entrance where you rung the bell by the wooden window, and it lifted to the bartender's face like a jack-in-the-box stuck sideways.

"Twenty-five cents worth o' the best," she'd say. Nothin' but the best for the Hennessys, and she, Ann Hennessy, was going to have the best of everything when she growed up, a lot more of the best than Ma ever had. She wasn't going to live in no dark rear house off Tenth Avenue, with the sink in the outside hall.

Washdays in that house everybody kept runnin' back and forth with buckets to fill the berlers on their wood-burning stoves. Mrs. Healy up on the top floor would scream, "Water, water — send up the water!" and Mrs. Shaughnessy would turn on her faucet all the harder to cut her to a trickle. With everybody seein' how everybody else's work was comin', takin' time out for the whiskey they called "a little sup," the wash hung over till Tuesday, Wednesday, Thursday— weren't never done.

All week they'd stand with big sticks, stirrin' the wash, plungin' their hands into the water, takin' 'em out red and steaming. Her hands weren't never goin' to look like theirs, she could promise you that, not her pretty, pale hands with the little veins like flower stems.

Ma's *best* used up so many quarters that she'd as leave give you a smack as a dime if ya needed it for somethin' special like a medal ribbon. Other kids at school was always winnin' medals, but this was about her first, not for no good marks, just for the paper angels she made to help decorate the schoolroom for Easter. You wore the medal on a ribbon round your neck till your week was up when you have it back to the Sisters with a new ribbon for whoever won it next.

Now if she was to ask for only fifteen cents worth of the best next time Ma sent her out with a quarter — oh no, she dasn't. Ma could easy tell, she'd beat her raw for the difference between fifteen and twenty-five cents worth. No — no, Ma knew her best. And suppose she did wise up. She was always knockin' her around for nothin', why not for somethin'?

A COUPLE OF DAYS before she was to give back the medal with a new ribbon, she started out with the wrapped bottle in its big market basket, a quarter held so tight it was a wonder it didn't work right into her palm. She knew she had the smile on her face that Ma wanted to beat out of her. "What ya always lookin' fer?" she'd say. "What ya expectin' out o' life?"

April damp could eat in but you wouldn't catch her hidin' her middy blouse under no outgrown coat — her big sister's middy with a red eagle on the sleeve. Her hair was nice and yella fallin' down about her white collar, the medal ribbon yella, too, pullin' at her hair, but nothin' like Ma would be pullin' it if she ever got wise.

"Fifteen cents worth," she told the bartender, "that's all Ma wants today — fifteen cents worth, and don't forget change of a quarter."

Before anything could happen to her dime, she went straight to Jacoby's store. Such ribbons — she set her basket down by the counter and just looked — reels and reels o' them, some wound tight, some open and ready to stream out to you in rivers of silk and satin. The counter was a garden o' ribbons. She wouldn't mind a bedroom without windas so much if she had all them ribbons fer light.

Yella like the watery sunlight on a row-boat up in Central Park, that was the one she wanted. No, the blue, all ripply like water at the docks just before she held her nose and jumped. She rain the tip of her nail along the grosgrain; stretched out a finger to a velvet redder than the rose on the lamp globe in the parlor; touched a satin that Ma's fingers would rough up.

That green so far down on the shelf she had to lean over the counter for a good look. That was it — that was her ribbon. She'd never set eyes on a green like that, not the lightest green lettuce, not even one of them fancy honeydews. It was yummy soft like green ice at a weddin', not that even. There was no green like it any-where— the green o' this ribbon.

"How much ya want fer it? Ten cents a yard?" she asked the clerk.

"Eighteen."

"Gimme ten cents worth."

"No odd lengths. We only sell yards and half yard."

"Well, would a half yard be long enough for a medal ribbon?"

"No, I'd say not."

"Mebbe a kid's neck?"

She lifted up her hair while the clerk tried the ribbon. His scissors snipped on the generous side of a half yard. The ribbon was hers.

Anything Ma could do to her, even if she was to put Pa up to beltin' her, it was worth it for this ribbon.

Pourin' water into that innocent whiskey was like puttin' water in somebody's veins — killin' 'em. In the basement sink down the block it took a lot of trickles to fill it up. Ma was in the parlor where she always had to receive the best, her apron off like the bottle was a visitor.

"What ya standin' back there fer?" Ma asked. "What ya scared of? I ain't gonna smack ya fer takin' all day."

Ma took the first swallow without suspicioning; then she began to taste her lips. "That ain't none o' the best," she said. "I'm goin' straight to Paddy's, and pour it down his throat."

"No — no — don't do that, Ma."

"And why not? Who're you to tell me what I won't do?"

"Well, you see, I — well, I needed a dime for a medal ribbon so bad that I just got fifteen cents worth and so's you'd have enough I added a smidgin of water —" She turned her head from the wallops that was sure to come, but then she had to peek out from her hair to see why they didn't.

"Let me see it," Ma said in a voice froze stiff as the water pipes in winter. "Let me see the ribbon."

Any minute Ma'd be knockin' her around, but still she couldn't help bein' a mite proud, holdin' out the ribbon — just what sunlight would be if it was green.

"So that's what it took for ya to sperl my best bit o' liquor — that cheap bit o' ribbon."

"Not cheap ribbon, Ma — the best."

"The best — I'll show ya yer cheap best."

Ma began pickin' at the ribbon — with her broken nails. "No, Ma — no —" Threads was all bustin' loose, leavin' a row stickin' up like a lot of grinning teeth.

"Ain't no best around here," Ma screamed at her. "You ain't gonna get no best in life no more'n I did — not as much. That hair'll never get ya no place; it's dirty egg yella. A pair of bright blue eyes won't do nothin' fer ya neither, not without a figger. You're wearin' your bones on the outside of yer skin, and no brains showin'. No, you're not goin' no place, you and yer cheap ribbon.

RIGHT THEN if she could've looked ahead and seen what was gonna happen to Ma, right then while her ribbon was nothin' but a bunch of cheap threads in Ma's hand, if she could just've looked ahead. Whenever she looked back, the two days was like one day, Ma tearin' her ribbon to nothin', and reachin' for a frozen clothesline, fallin' outa the window, all twisted when she hit — dead before anybody got to her. She'd never die like that down there — die like Ma with nothin' of the best.

The ways outa Hell's Kitchen wasn't many, just like Ma said. Roller skatin' up Dreamland she met fellas enough, but they wasn't goin' no place. A couple girl friends was askin' fer the skid way out. "Who wants ta go straight when it's Tenth Avenue" Lola kept sayin, only she went for a whiz of a skater who never got no further than Hoboken. As for her own self, she couldn't of faced Sister Mary Frances without she done things regular. Besides, she weren't never asked.

The Sisters kept tellin' her she'd get places by studyin' hard, but she could never sit still long enough. Maybe it was on account of always bein' ready to scram out of Pa came home fightin' drunk. And who wanted to pucker over a stingy little page when you could swing a bat in a vacant lot, skin off to the docks, or look in all them fancy windas across town? If she hadn't come near dyin' of typhus, her 'stead of her sister Agnes could have had a year in a convent the time Pa was doin' good.

The job she could get wasn't much. What she wanted was to be a buyer in a big department store, getting' paid fer buyin' the best of everything. She got a start in Altman's sewin' room. Maybe she wouldn't of been canned fer botchin' the job is she'd done like she should in Sister Ursula's sewin' class. The ward Captain got her a few jobs that didn't amount to nothin', mostly in rush times like sortin' Christmas mail.

Then she met Frank at one of them political shindigs. She thought he was goin' places when she married him. Nobody could've tried harder to make somethin' of hisself, runnin' an elevator nights, studyin' days. The doctor said all that work, half starvin' hisself, getting' no sleep, made him take sick of TB.

All the while she worked her hands to blisters cleanin' at the YW so close by she could run back and forth lookin' after Frank, she kept seein' her green ribbon ripped to shreds — seein' it in a lousy bit of wash on the line, on filthy scraps of paper blowin' down the street — on all the cleanin' rags in her hands, on the tattered handkerchiefs Frank'd cough into, coughin' his life away.

Frank's passing should've meant more to her than an end to heavy cleanin'. Maybe it did — she was too tired to know. Sister Mary Margaret helped her with the ad that was to change things for her. "Woman, light cleaning," Sister Mary Margaret wanted to write. "No, Sister, not just woman — I want to try for a fine neighborhood. Couldn't ya say, 'Lady — refined — desires light housework, full or part time'?"

Part-time was about all anybody wanted, maybe on account of always bein' in such a hurry to please that she kept breakin' things. Anyway she was good on the touches — setting' a doll on a pillor real cute, arrangin' things just so, changin' the furniture better, only most everybody was set in their ways like her sister Agnes. She couldn't keep from fixin' things either even if her ideas weren't of the best, like the time she was too free with the erl can and damaged Mrs. Eggers' Oriental. Her paint always crackled, her stains and varnishes never took, her clamps wouldn't never hold.

All them women wanted of her was cleanin' — no use trying to keep her nails long and the polish they give her from peelin' — ya just couldn't clean and keep lookin' your best to yer fingertips. Her eyes bein' what they was, everyone followed her around when she cleaned, yet she couldn't bring herself to hide the bright blue of her eyes behind glasses when her hair was so dingy grey. Her smile kept her young lookin', too. Everybody said it was like she was always expectin' somethin' nice to happen. And maybe she didn't have Ma's figger, but it was still slim as a young girl's. She was always took fer ten years younger than her sister Agnes 'sted of four years older.

Agnes was a widow, too — by desertion — that's what come of hangin' around the docks eyein' them seamen. When Frank passed on, her and Agnes moved in a coupla blocks from where they were born. Agnes oughta been a lady with them bird bones of hers, and she was always ailing' like one — Lydia E. Pinkham things wrong.

Durin' the war you could begin to feel a mite important with everybody after you, trustin' ya with all kinds of things. Mrs. Leighton, the little G.I. bride who lived in a fine neighborhood just off Washington Square, let her take care of Wendy when the child was a newborn bit o' pinkness, her lips puffed out to a tiny open rose for her bottle.

Much as she wanted to give of her best to Wendy, the bonnets she made for her didn't shape right, the panties wound up with no proper seat, the carriage wheel she fixed fell off. Each new thing she did was going to be the best, but somethin' always went wrong. The best just wasn't in her.

In them fine apartment buildings across town she'd had lots o' luxuries. Mrs. Prentice gave her the use of the bathtub sometimes, encouragin' her to bathe in bubbles that made her smell like the best of 'em. Heat steamin' up in the radiators, snowy refrigerators, stoves with pilot lights, all those things were hers most the day.

The clothes everybody give her had the best labels — Bonwit's, Saks, Bergdorf Goodman. Just so she wouldn't feel like charity she'd juggle around what didn't fit good, the Lily Daché hat to Mrs. Leighton only it landed on Wendy's head as a play hat, the Tailored Woman suit to Mrs. Prentice. Some got huffy when she'd give 'em things, maybe the others didn't like it neither only they was too perlite ta say.

P EOPLE in them fine buildins' was nice to you without lettin' you be friends. Oh, they did enough: tickets to shows, even a locked-in box at Carnegie once, but never when they was along. You was given all kinds of cherce food without never bein' invited to sit. Christmas gifts was just money tips or somethin' they couldn't use, wrapped up in a hurry. When she gave them gifts she tried to see what was needed if only a pot holder. And for Sylvia — Mrs. Leighton — she couldn't help thinkin' of her as Sylvia — she give presents a little beyond her pocketbook like the eight-day clock, and for Wendy all the things she'd never had, a real doll carriage 'stead of a shoe box, dolls with eyes that opened and shut, not a cloth-covered soap strainer.

Whenever she hung around after hours at the Leightons to play with Wendy, help out in any way she could or just chat, she felt Mrs. Leighton almost wished she would clear out. Sylvia — Mrs. Leighton — could've been bewitched by a leprechaun the way she looked past you, through you, never at you till you never knew how ya stood with her, whether she had any idea you just wanted to be a friend.

This wind went right through you. She should've worn the sealskin Mrs. Prenctice gave her no matter how ratty it looked. No amount of sweaters under the Bonwit coat could make it warm enough for winter. She patted the folds of her carry-all. No duty gift in there, no money tip. She was thought well enough of to be given one of the six photographs of Sylvia and Wendy — thought more than well of — thought of it as it was signed. "To our friend, Ann."

"Oh, Mrs. Leighton — Wendy," she'd said. "you're the best."

Woolworth's wasn't good enough for the frame she was goin' to buy when she got paid. She'd go to Wanamaker's, the store that was elegant down on Broadway since she was a kid buyin' one piece of Reagan's best candy 'stead o' the big bag of cough drops he give ya fer a nickel.

If it wasn't fer the wind blowin' all that filth down Tenth Avenue, she'd take a look at her darlins' this instant. It was so cold it made yer eyes water. Them clothes down her street would freeze on the line fer sure. Good to step into her own hallway, even dark and smelly like it was. Her stomach give a turn at the thick stink of erl stoves mixed in with stale fry. The air in their own apartment was nice and fresh with that Airwick what was supposed ta be the green chlorophyll of plants. Agnes had no business calllin' it a waste o' good money.

No sooner did she take a coupla spice cakes outa her bag and set 'em on a best plate than Agnes lit into her. "Them expensive cakes again. Why you could've bought a dozen spice cookies for what them two cost."

"Not much I couldn't. Them's French."

"Just the same, will you kindly leave the marketing to me? You've no buyin' sense at all."

Agnes was makin' them little smackins' with her lips like she always did when she thought she was bestin' ya, smackin' away like she was tastin' a sweet That smack trap o' hers was worse'n Ma's hair-pulllins'.

"What about the bottle yer always nursin'?"' she give it back to Aggie. "Not just twenty-five cents worth o' the best — a whole bottle with a fancy label."

"Keep yer verce down, can't you? You're not playin' in the street."

Funny thing, her and Agnes was both a piece o' Ma, both wantin' the best, only Agnes never dast try fer it. That's why Aggie couldn't stand the smile on her face no more'n Ma could.

The muscatel Mrs. Eggers give her, she'd set it on the table along with the spice cakes. "Let's have a little sup," she said to Agnes, a bit proudly.

"Celebratin' what, might I ask?"

"You'll see — you'll see." Real careful-like, she drew out the pitcher of Wendy and her mother, opened out the elegant cover, white like a weddin', and set it on the table full in the afternoon light — the mother lookin' down at Wendy, her head curved like the Blessed Virgin, and Wendy reachin' out to her Mama Ann.

"Read it — read what it says — 'To our friend, Ann' — they think of me as a real friend."

"Dontcha know that's just an autographin' custom? Any beauty parlor or barber shop's got picthers autographed, 'To my friend.' Don't mean a thing."

"But them pitchers cost so much she only ordered six of 'em, and give one to me."

"Knowin' you, I'm sure you done plenty o' hintin' — probably come right out and asked. Why, Mrs. Leighton won't even let Wendy come up here — thinks she'll get sperled food, and germs, and pneumonia from a cold water flat."

She was Ma tearin' at the green ribbon, tearin' it to nothin'. All them clotheslines outside the winda, she could wish, she could almost wish...

"And don't go spendin' money on no fancy frame. You and yer best."

[*The American Mercury*, July 1950]

CONTENTS OF A LADY'S HANDBAG

OFFICE CAN WAIT, a noon this misting, with autumn hanging onto summer like the Park seals to their sun ledge. Furred in by odor of seal pond and jungle cage, he waited for the keeper to come sloshing his pail of fish.

Point poising her sheathed umbrella, a woman stretched up on her wine-suede shoes. His wife would look like a panda beside her — the panda and the heron. Dark silk coat in leaf whisperings. Late thirties, he'd guess, like him the long-boned elegance, never young, never old.

Golden brown suede, a handbag under her arm — all the ingenious shapes of women's handbags, picnic hampers, feed bags, saddle rolls, hoboes' bundle — this one long and narrow, stretched smooth as her skin. A woman's handbag is the woman. Some carry them heavy burden, others swing them light, open them wide, edge them open. Contents of a lady's handbag — the secret contents.

Seals leaped auking to the fish, pail heaped like his incoming mail basket. Other men around the office could lengthen their lunch hour, but let a traffic manager be a couple of minutes late and he jammed interstate commerce.

The woman whispered her silk against him poising to the seals. His smile just missed — not that she turned to see — missed the way his face just missed, had thickened and spread in the hardening. His wife's face just missed, too, sugared past prettiness. Ralphie and little Helen in her image, Jeff in his.

The woman's handbag, so loosely held in her leaning forward, he could see the flower carved crystal of the clasp. No more noticed him than did the tall girls back in dancing school days when he crossed to them for partners. Reasonable height now — skin still too oily.

In the crowd about the seals, the woman shouldn't be letting her handbag slip away — someone might — his hand went out to secure it for her, but as if by reflex he held it in his hand. Quick under his topcoat, before anyone could mistake him for a thief. She felt the slipping away, looked down at her feet, backed away for a better search, too well-bred to panic, glanced at those around her with guarded suspicion, quickened her heel-beat almost to a run up the steps to the terrace cafeteria. He walked up the hill past the bear cages, their stench unbearable as the pressure to unclasp the crystal to within.

Rock hollow roofed by golding sycamores — he slipped in under, tented the golden suede in his topcoat, opened. To lining untouched as bridal satin, contents in garden order as if waiting for this moment. Everything sheathed —comb, mirror, compact. The lining held her scent, citrus cool. Business cards from textile houses — swatches of material. Her purse plump with bills — six ones, three fives — eighty-seven cents in change. For her, the issue should be new issue, the coins still in mint frost. A beat bobby pin, the one disorder. What had she tried to pry open? Or had it bent with her weight of hair?

Inner compartment. He felt in the deep satin to tissue whisperings, like her silk coat. Air-mail letter — Rhoda Bascombe, One Stuyvesant Oval. Something about meeting on a cruise. Could he take her to dinner and the theater? Too formal for her, she needed impulse like his taking her purse.

He pocketed the cash, as was only practical. How far could she get without so much as bus fare? She'd be all right, she could cab collect. Her tiny noon needed upside-downing. Let her adventure into what it's like to be caught in mink midtown without a dime, rethink the right and wrong of theft, and taught her not to be too trusting, reminded her that the world hungers, forced her to think of him. After she had lost count of Dresden dull days, she would live this. Her thoughts were nothing about contents of her handbag. How many bills? Much change? What papers? All the losses of her life nothing to the immediacy of this loss, rather, all her losses were folded into this one loss — he had reached her being.

Customary, he's read, to get rid of the evidence. Not the trash can, not her golden suede, the clear satin. He kept a tiny matchbox encrusted with seashells and sequins; covered over the bag with its crystal clasp with a gold fall of leaves.

In going through his pockets for the dry cleaner, Helen dug out the matchbox. "Wherever did you get this?" She jogged it on a palm used to kitchen matches. *Her* handbag stuffed shapeless with the children's things, disintegrated cleaning tissues, somewhat soiled comb, tag ends of make-up.

"Can't rightly recall how I came by it. The office, I suppose — somebody must have left it on my desk."

"I like pretty extras too, but we need so many —"

A bit of glitter dust rubbed off on his fingers as he pocketed the sequined box.

THE PARK turned mirror, drawing the fire of his thoughts wherever he lunched, walked. He crossed to the Sixth Avenue entrance, one noon, not letting his feet take the path to the rock hollow where the smooth-stretched suede was covered over.

In the crackle of autumn sun, he lay on the browning grass by lunch-hour picnickers. A group of office girls were opening paper bags, biting into sandwiches, their pocketbooks on grass and rock ledge — cheap plastics, see-through, vinyl, miniature picnic hampers and bird cages left over from summer, some with appalling encrustations. One, plaid shaped like a tam o' shanter, had pert appeal, but the contents would be like the others: Blue Cross, Social Security, safety pins, deposit slips on harsh dyed synthetics sleazing away on the shelf before they were even paid for.

He got up, brushed himself off, and walked deeper into the park, coming to a rock-crested hill. A tot was throwing autumn leaves up over her head. Little boys played cops and robbers among the rock sparklers, a man dozed with his shoes off. Down slope, a woman was lying on her cashmere coat reading a book, her hair in a red-gold pile about to tumble from its pine. Her handbag a roll of oak-brown leather, its brass hinges reinforcing the secrets within.

Settling to the slope, he unfolded his newspaper to the page where he had left off reading on the subway. He inched closer, his paper a shadow triangle across the waiting leather. What was he doing, he, Kenneth M. Cranston, snake-crawling the grass in the manner of park thieves? Handbag all but sliding into his hand, that was one thing, but *this*? — His brain might as well be a squirrel chase in the branches above for all it did to keep him from spreading out the newspaper. His heart beat hard enough to hear, as he drew the sun-warmed leather under his armpit. The snake crawled down the slope.

Just as he got up to go, she screeched, "My bag! my bag!" too grackle-voiced for her red gold hair, the leather rich roll inside his coat.

"Boys — boys — you give me back my handbag this minute." She ran up the rocks, grackling, "Stop them — somebody stop them!" Such cheap hysterics, her bag might as well be cheap plastic. Nothing he wanted. Far enough away, he concealed it in the folds of his newspaper and dropped it for bad fish in the garbage can.

Monkey chattering to himself that this bad experience should cure him, he kept from the park on autumn days when it was a golden Circe willowing its arms to him.

THEN, A DAY dropped down out of frost talons to early autumn warmth. The smell of civet and seal weighting the breezes, he crossed the plaza, went with the leaf dance along the walk to the seal pond. Handbags loose held in the pressing forward, none worth taking.

Up the steps a girl was sitting in the wing curve of a stone eagle, her bag at its base. Exciting, unbearable promise starting sweat from his pores. Ambitious reach of blonde leather for a miss small enough to crawl into the eagle's wings. More like a dispatch case. Mirror-lidded? Or did it hide a modest glass? Pretty witty Nelly face, as she looked up a blue balloon caught in the branches like a bubble of sky. Her pump swings, loose at the heel as if she wanted to kick it off, kick up to the blue.

He sat behind her at the base of the eagle. Quick, under his coat. Started down the crowded zoo walk, jumped a balloon on a stick at a rusted voice in his ear, "Clumsy snatch, my boy." He tightened against the bag under his armpit. "Relax — I'm no copper." Darning needle of a man sharping his features at him. "You amateurs — A snatch-and-grab like you got me pinched in a store once, just by staring after me."

"I got away, didn't I?"

"Dames is too noisy, their pokes too bulky for what's in 'em. If you gotta grift dames, shade yer duke, grift only in a crowd, grift fast. Never stare at the poke yer after. With a little practice, you might be a cannon. You don't stir up no suspicion — you look like a sucker yourself."

"Cannon?"

"Sure — one of us. Most of us won't have nothin' to do with you snatch-and-grabs."

"Who do you recruit? Juvenile delinquents?"

"Naw. Slum kids don't have the front us pros need. You gotta know how to fast-talk. Hotel people make good pros, the kind what hides us for a cut. Maybe you and me could boost the stores. I got an angle. Stupid salesgirls leave their pokes in drawers behind the counter. Rich haul, pay days."

"Not me. I go my own way."

"You won't get no fix when you need it if you stay snatch-and-grab. A cannon almost never gets pinched, can't afford the time out. Should it happen, he can make a deal on the way to the precinct unless he runs into an ornery copper, and that's where the fix comes in. But mostly it's the amateur what gets booked."

"No thanks — the park's for me in my own style."

"O.K., sucker, but if you change your mind, just look for me at Whitey's behind the Coliseum. Right now, you'd better ditch the evidence. With that arm clutch, any copper'd spot it under your coat. See you around, only don't give me the eye."

Easing his grip on the vanity under his armpit, he walked on out of the park to a cafeteria men's room, locked the door of his cubicle, and opened the blonde calf on its wide-swinging hinges to a mirror lid that startled his own spread features back to him.

Flowered silk cosmetic case, theatre tickets, a silver feather earring, phone number on a card board coaster, scratched across a memo, *Niles is a noodlehead, Niles is a noodlehead.* Three dollar bills and a dollar-sixty-six in change. He kept the money to be sensible, slipped the earring into his inner pocket. If Helen should happen on the silver feather, well, he *found it.*

HELD OFF THE PARK until a deadness of winter fit only for dog walkers, a snow blue twilight after work, he drift-plunged and path-slid up to Pilgrim where the youngsters banged down their sleds beneath the bronze Pilgrim on his pedestal, watched until the lights started up like yellow birds across the hills and hollows.

A woman in leopard skin, Brunnhilde of a woman, set down her leopard bag on the base of the monument to give a little boy's sled a push. All too reflex he had the bag under his arm, and was back to path before her voice at his ear, "I'll trouble you for my handbag." No Brunnhilde voice, more Mimi.

"Are you addressing me by any chance?"

"Who else?"

"You think that I --"

"Now don't say *Do I look the kind?* What is the kind? You can't all look like Peter Lorre."

"What are you going to do?"

"The police are all in where it's warm, toasting their tootsies, but there's a call box near by."

"Here —" he handed her the leopard.

"Look, if you're that desperate, I can give you something to tide you over. You don't have to steal from me — I give."

"No — no, I don't need it —"

"Call it a loan if you like —"

"No — "

"Whenever you're tempted to steal, remember, the person is probably only too willing to help out —" she gaped her handbag to a plump purse.

"No — I mean, no —" He outdistanced her down the ash-sprinkled path, tightened at a police call box as if the bag were still under his arm, saw leopard spots in the lighted snow.

Winter and her gaped face, her gaped bag did in all desire to walk the park. Work so far behind he often had his lunch sent in. Handbags still took his glance. As some men's went straight to the ankle, and on from there, he started with the handbag. All the hints— no end to the imaginings.

A DAY OF MARCH wind, he crossed Columbus Circle, went into the park a ways. Red lifted his eyes to a rock where a girl leaned back on her hands, face to the sun wind. Her hair discreetly wild, moderate hoops through her ears, red shoes, Valentine of a red envelope bag, on the rock beside her. He went around the curve of the path, climbed the hill to the back of her rock. Women's carelessness your best partner, the cannon had said, *Quick — quick as a cinder in the eye.* Reached without shading his duke. Hand gripped from above, voice blooding, "Officer! Officer!—"

Knew better than to make a run for it. A cop started up the hill as if he had been in camouflage just below. "What's the trouble here?"

"This man tried to steal my handbag."

"I like that. Do I look like a common thief? Do I?"

"That's not the point, officer. He —"

"Courtesy certainly is dangerous in a public park. Your handbag was sliding off the rock, and I only tried to retrieve it for you."

"Well, lady, what do you want to do?" the officer paused.

"What can I say but *forget it?* I did have it at a precarious slant, and if you were just being gallant, I'm sorry, I truly am. Thank you— thank you both —" She high-heeled down the slope, her slippery red envelope sliding back a bit from her arm.

Warned off spring at its windy start, warned just as the light was beginning to pattern noonday dreamers, handbags bright as Easter eggs across the grass. From Fifty-seventh street he could see the bouffant windows, the pink and white flowering.

A S THE DAYS steamed hot enough to curl the edges of spring, he walked under park sycamores on the other side of the wall.

After work, one sizzler, he turned back at the mouth of the subway to walk under the cool of the trees, let a willow soft-talk him over the wall, to lie in the chlorophyll breezes.

On his elbow he watched the cool handbags, the silks and straws, glazed kids; closed his mind to their contents, even the white linen on the grass within reach. He got up fast, brushed off, walking toward the boating lake, stood above the esplanade, cooling his gaze to the fountain below, half closed his eyes to the sound of horse and carriage, heard the silks of Victorian women, saw their drawstring bags at wrist and belt, on the steps by carvings in stone, the green of olives, cool of limes.

Starting down by the lake along the path that steeped and curved by the stone-carved steps, he smelled a sweetness close to honeysuckle except that it was more citrine. A woman in white linen — her cologne — white and tangerine delicate as Japanese lanterns, her glove-soft bag on the ledge of the balustrade to unfasten the leash. He reached pro fast, sheltered the tangerine folds under his jacket, walked along the willowed bank of the lake toward the boathouse.

Glaced kid so cool, soft and fragrant, he rubbed it against his cheek in the men's room, worked the intricate clasp, opening it up and out to the petal folds of deep blue satin, a purse of the same satin containing only a key. Comb-case, compact, lipstick in matching enamels, a Roman coin pill box. Dog biscuits. Snapshots of a far-away child on a palm-circled beach. In the deepest corner of satin, a button for his inner pocket, a tiny button of mother-of-pearl.

OUR REV.

THE NEW REV. looks like somethin' outa Exodus in his coat of dirty fleece, hair bushin' up black whilst it's oily enough to be anointed, them eyes of his burnin' with Hell or Holy Fire. Hernandez-Coronadas by name, and powerful particular about partin' it in the middle.

Coronadas was down in Mexico studyin' to be a Priest when he seen our light. How we come to call him to our United Church here in Mango has to do with what we was prepared to pay. After Seth Hawes, our *Rev.* for bettern'n forty year, passed into the Heavenly Kingdom that his preachin' always made cozy as a rockin' chair, we had eighteen months of supply pastors, none findin' our little upstate town temptin' at a yearly $2,000.

The Superintendent of our State Conference informs us that we can get Coronadas for only $1,500 while warnin' us he's no bargain at any price. "Either he makes good in his next pulpit," says the Super, "or we'll give him back to the Catholics."

In our church, we do the hirin' and firin', ain't nobody tells us what to do, not even our Super. As President of the Pulpit Committee, I got Coronadas for $1,300 bein' he has a bad accent and not much future. Even at that figger he give us such a sample of his preachin' that we ain't got over it yet, his words kind of, well, elegant, like a carpet layin'.

Day we tried to make the Coronadas feel to home in the parsonage, him and the Missus and the five kids, it was like movin' in the Indian Reservation. Injun rugs, baskets, pottery, heathen figgers in clay. Canvases, stacks of 'em, high as boards in my lumber yard, canvases we was supposed to baby along like seedlings at his heel-clickin' commands as we hoisted.

The stiff-spined little coot communicates with his squaw by thumb jerks. Come, she comes; tote, she totes; hind, she'd hind. Her braid-wound head, snappin' back like branches after a gunblast, jumps the kids into line. Whilst the men might like the knack, it's goin' to rile up our women.

Chances are, we wouldn't warm to nobody after losin' Seth Hawes. He was a right *Rev.*, one to lend a hand, whether sawin' away at a big spruce with my men, fightin' fires other than Hell, or pitchin' hay.

Now we don't expect no fellow as book-read as Coronadas to sweat with us, but when you give him a load of lumber to fix his floorin' and replace termited beams, you don't expect him to leave it out to rot. Guess if I'd plumped some adobe down, he'd of gotten to work.

Take Jed, he comes down with his tractor to plow the *Rev's* patch only to be thumb-jerked off the place, Coronadas allowin' he's no Martha busy 'bout many things…

★ ★ ★

AIN'T MAKIN' no mention of what I see Wednesday, save to this here scratch pad. I was deliverin' a load of lumber down at the Indian Reservation, Miss Spriggs and Mrs. Phelps ridin' with me, charity bent, when we see why the *Rev's* been neglectin' us of late. Him and the Missus wasn't visitin' out of no charity, but they was enjoyin' their selves with all the injun blood in 'em, the Missus weavin' rugs, and the *Rev*. makin' flat-faced clay idols.

That ain't all. I come on him behind the woodshed later, with some injun girl, his hand where it hadn't ought to be. Bein' a good Christian, I won't say nothin' about this, and, besides, I got more'n one woodshed of my own…

The rugs the Missus wove at such times showed up in the Sanctuary — vultures, bird gods and all — Coronadas tellin' us that moth and dust doth corrupt our Church carpets more'n what's fittin'. Well, what was done on the new rugs wasn't fittin' neither. "Dancing out praises at the altar is a glory of worship most pleasing to the Almighty," says Coronadas, "or He wouldn't set the leaves and the grasses and the waves to dancing nor plan a rhythm of tides and seasons and stars."

His Missus, dressed in what looks to be a nightgown, gets up before the altar with her arm dancin', braids snakin' down her back. After all, when you bargain for a minister, the wife's part of the package; you expect her to help out in Sunday school, at church suppers and the like, not go off on no dancin' toot.

The followin' Sunday, she has our soprano throwin' her weight around, and the junior choir choir millin' about, holdin' up bowls of plenty, in what the town librarian says is one of them fertilizer dances.

When the juniors start worshippin' with their flanks, Mrs. Innes grabs her daughter out of that there group right in the midst of the service. Other mothers motion their kids down, somebody pulls the organ plug, and that was a stop to dancin' in the Sanctuary for good and all.

Coronadas's preachin' has us on the fence. Mebbe it's good; mebbe it ain't. Might as well be listenin' to a Latin mass at times for all we could make out, more like music than Gospel. Fact is, he's preachin' past us to them big city churches what never hear. And we was willin' to take him on, accent and all. Coronadas is a two-headed preacher anyhow, one lifted to heaven, the other on our necks, like his sermon at Mrs. Innes: "Are you a battle-axe?" Us men went for it till that toy poodle what scarce sprung his hair above the pulpit knocked off each an' every one in squirmin' turn, called me a dirty capitalist for not lettin' my men make fools of theirself joinin' no union when I pay 'em proper.

Leastways, them sermons was words; others was his paintin's held up — burls, knotholes, and shavin's the blame things looked like to me. "Inner essence of the Kingdom," says Coronadas, "an advanced look at the picture Bible I've been working on seventeen years."

With the *Rev's* buttin' in every place, we can't so much as call the church windas our'n. He knocks out the blue panes, and starts makin' stained glass ones which sounds well and good till he has the Holy Family lookin' Mexican.

Our *Rev.*, we likes to be one of us, or leastways carin' what comes of us. Preachin's a job to him with no time and a half for overtime like when our late-widowed Mrs. Eakins knocked on his door at an hour when decent folks is through supper. Coronadas comes flappin' out like a bat, screamin': "Can't we even enjoy our meals? Must you swim through our digestive juices like an amoeba?"

Any town that can get Methodists and Presybyterians to unite should digest Coronadas, but believe me, we're sore tried like Job. Jeff Guerney says, "It's B.C.-D.C. with us — before Coronadas, during Coronadas, and if he ain't careful, it'll soon be A.C." Every fool hobby comes ahead of us. He's always off to the city for books and artist's supplies, lectures and concerts and theaters, peddlin' his picture Bible among the publishers, most-like tryin' for a city pulpit what the Super says ain't for him. Moses got his big moment on a mountain top, but Coronadas has to find his on city streets. Mango is in the sticks, all right, but he has to say so sad, "out in the *little* sticks," them wild eyes of his lookin' for a chariot of fire down our street.

When he does stay in Mango, he's either in a mess of paint and clay, or he has the house full of injuns, fills our pews with 'em, as if they didn't have no church of their own, or he's makin' up to the town characters, the hermit squattin' on Stebbins' old place, and Silvernail, the mural painter, one of them returned city smears what never goes to church. Which brings me to the R.C. business.

"Comparison shoppin'" Mrs. Bowman calls it when he goes to t'other end of town to chew the fat with Father Degnan.

Anyway, after what Coronadas says the R.C. church's done to Mexico, here he is tryin' to put in some of their methods, stinkin' up the place with incense when we like the smell of the open fields just outside, the pine grove, and the good old church timbers. He shows up in a Roman collar, and sets the choir to chantin'; suggests a fund-raisin' lottery when most of our folks think gamblin' sinful as drink. He won't sign no pledge card against smokin' and drinkin' on account of he'd rather get high on Father Degnan's wine and go chantin' through the streets after ten o'clock at night, every blessed word Latin. And he keeps a wine cellar in the potato bin for the visitin' monks what keep turnin' the parsonage into one of them retreats.

It's getting' so we need a mine detector before every step, like the confessional he put over on us at a Wednesday evening get-together what turns out to be truth or consequences only it has to be Truth. Soul searchin' the *Rev.* calls it when it's just a means of getting' us into a room-size confession box. Them meetins' was popular, all right, before we begun to get the drift. The fun of talkin' about ourself plus getting' an ear what others is up to crowded in folks like it was the County Fair, cars parked right as a log jam.

Motion was made, and seconded by us members of the Board that Jed Yates speak to Coronadas concernin' what the Reformation was all about. "We're Protestant," she says to Coronadas, givin' the word its protest sound. "If you ain't *protested* all the way, you better go back where you came from."

CORONADAS erupts like that volcano what appeared in the Mexican cornfield. "I reassert my right to protest, protest, protest," he says. "I take this privilege so seriously that I claim the right to protest against the protestants, themselves, if need be. *Viewpoint liberal* is what I set down on my ministerial record. Then let me *be* liberal!" He goes on spoutin' all the things that made the pulpit committee shine to him in the first place. "You people build characters" — *character*, he must of meant — "you confess ecumenicity. Let me be ecumenical. If you but knew it, I'm a walking ad for you. Never let me live to regret that I am your convert."

That's just it — he's always makin' Mango feel it's got to show him …

★ ★ ★

AIN'T NO LIMIT to that fellow's gall. This time he hits us in our pocketbooks, which is really hittin' below the belt. The slicker is into us for the amount of $2,200 by borrowin' fifty here, a hundred there, four hundred from yours truly, makin' each of us think he was the only one he ever come to. He tells us it's a small loan against the check he'll be gettin' from his publishers for that there Picture Bible. Come to find he ain't got no publisher, and Silvernail says ain't like to have. That $2,200 ain't countin' the $490 grocery bill he run up at Trenkle, and the thousands of dollars worth of furniture he bought on the installment plan.

Why, the fellow lives better'n what we do. A houseman, if you please, somebody up from the city workin' mostly for board and learnin'. Ain't nobody around here'd be a houseman in a white coat; sounds a mite too Episcopal anyhow. Coronadas sends him down to Trenkle for groceries too fancy for Mango; demands they be special ordered; smells up the town with heathen cookin'. And in that pigsty he has stuff what Silvernail says would start any art dealer dickerin'.

Upshot is, them bills brings the State Head down on us when all we ask is *Leave us be.* Ain't nobody tells us what to do, not even the Super, except we're into the State Conference for a loan to repair the steeple and wantin' hundreds more for runnin' water. When that fool, Coronadas, has to go and treat the Conference like some sort of daddy to foot his bills. Whereupon the Super says we better get rid of Coronadas on account of the Conference won't be responsible for a one of his debts. "And I can promise you I'll never recommend him for another pastorate in this or any other Association," the Super declares.

"Why, I call that downright unchristian," says Jed Yates.

Christian — unchristian. Them words is buzzin' in my mind like a saw. Unchristian to bounce him? Fat lot Coronadas ever taught us about bein' Christian, shovin' us around like he did, preachin' up in the clouds or down his nose.

With the board meetin' Friday I'm wrastlin' with myself which ways to vote. Maybe I'm somethin' of a camel stuck in the needle's eye like the *Rev.* says, but I ain't unchristian enough to blacklist a fellow right out of his livelihood.

A day or so before the meetin', me and Pete Bainbridge, the school principal, got to talkin' about bein' Christian. "Here's a man who comes to us in spiritual need," says Bainbridge, "looking to us to show *him* the way. We'll never accomplish that by ousting him."

Well and good for thinkin' folk like ourselves, but what all those others he cut down? Thing is, we each secret felt the other deserved what he got. "A true minister holds up a mirror as well as a torch," says Bainbridge, as we go around tryin' to stir up Christian feelin' towards the *Rev.* amongst them he called boobs and battle-axes.

With the Super rowin' around, and us talkin' in corners, the little family sees what's comin'. They'd be hittin' the road again, leavin' most everything behind for their creditors, savin' his paintings. Them he offered up in payment for his personal debts. Some let him keep the paintins' like they was lettin' a beggar keep his pencils. A few of us what what'd gone deeper into Christian thinkin' took 'em so he'd think he was some shakes with the paint brush.

His kids go wanderin' about like they give up all hope of ever havin' a place of their own where they can eat regular, not that we wouldn't be glad to get rid of the five of 'em. The way Coronadas keeps 'em down, they sneak their mischief whilst open fellows like my Steve gets the blame. Mebbe the tribe might buck up with a feel of belongin' some place. "We been warming our seats instead of our hearts," Mrs. Todd came out with in spite of his sendin' back the pie she cooked at a church supper like he was at a restaurant.

When the Super sees he ain't getting' no place he hops up the line, leavin' us to decide one way or t'other. Board's meetin' up at Derwenter's place, one of our boys what went citified without quite takin' the country out of him. Meantime I'm doin' some last-minute collarin'…

★ ★ ★

WHAT WENT ON at that board meetin' is somethin' for the scratch pad. We sit around Derwenter's fire, drinkin' hot cider and soundin' off. "Let's show *that* heathen we're better Christians that what he is," I tell 'em, "and take him for better or worser."

Fred Wicks spits his tobacco juice short of the logs like he always does when he's goin' to vote contrary.

Trenkle, what's cash-and-carry from here on, know where to aim at Wicks. "You ain't never goin' to see the color of your money if you bounce him, but if he's under our eye when he sells a paintin' or gets his pitcher Bible published, we can collect what's comin' to us. He must have some art in him to be that screw-jawed."

"If we start kickin' folks out of Mango for bein' different," says Miss Spriggs, perchin' her librarian pencil above a pad as if she was renewin' Coronadas like a book, "why, we'd have to get rid of most the town."

"Besides," says Jenkins, what knows all about sports from his dairy breedin', "Mango might be kind of dead without the *Rev.*"

"But he ain't no Christian," says Fred Wicks, spittin' short again, tobacco juice sizzlin' bitter on the stone. "Fact is, we're the ones what has to be Christian to get along with him."

"Well, if he's makin' us better Christians, he's doin' what we called him for," says Jenkins.

"But without knowin' he's doin' it," says Wicks. "That ain't right."

Trenkle's grim wrinkles him up like one of Wicks's prize squashes. "Then we're bein' Christian for him, and should be the ones collectin' his salary."

"What Mr. Trenkle means to convey," says Miss Spriggs, "is that it's up to us to be shepherds to our one black sheep."

"Ain't so good ourself we can go kickin' out the *Rev.*," Says Jenkins. "Ain't never fixed his furnace, ain't repaired his roof, ain't rid the church attic of no bats, nor its beams of hornets, and there's some even wished one of them hornets would sting him on the mouth like it done with the supply *Rev.*"

"Where will they go? Who will call them?" Miss Spriggs opens out her arms like one of them *Give* posters.

"The man come to us," said Pete Bainbridge, "to our United Church, and we're elected to show him the way. Christianity is on the spot right now throughout the world. How did a handful of ragged Christians in a pagan land turn it Christian in the first place? They lived such shining lives that everyone wanted to know their secret — follow the Way."

Derwenter reached down a Bible from the mantle, huntin' for a passage, then read: "This is my commandment, That ye love one another, as I have loved you."

Them words never sounded so shined up as what they done right when we was livin' 'em.

★ ★ ★

BEFORE WE TINKER with a fellow's life," says Jenkins," "we better do a little prayin'." We bow our heads, and Pete Bainbridge prays, "Father, show us the Christian way towards our Reverend. Let us never cause him to regret that he has sought Thee through our church. Help us to accept this stranger, and make him friend. May he feel secure in our love."

Somethin' comes over us in our prayin', somethin' like the feeling of the Disciples at some first meetin' place after the Master had gone on, like we was Christians alone for the first time, layin' down the first rules, livin' Christ, His love. Anyway, we was new-born in our faith.

And we went out into the Congregation, and spread the word, and by the time the Super got back from whatever trouble shootin' he done up the line, we was lettin' Coronadas know he come to the right place. We voted him a new furnace; wiped out his debts; I even proposed raisin' him to 1,500. Coronadas is in, he's ours — our *Rev.*

[*The American Mercury*, March 1953]

BEGGAR BY NAME

HOLDING down this desk meant holding it against a feeling that it was on the rise like a séance table. His secretary was in her own state of suspension, a rose under glass.

Miss Macallum, he'd like to say to her, Miss Macallum, did you know that I was a beggar on the streets before Hendricks exorcised his particular devils by shoving me into this job? Had approached Hendricks as just another likely face ... "You know this man's town. What would you do if you'd landed a job just as you were down to your last cent?"

"Why, Nat Reardon. We used to be junior copywriters together, remember? Must have been some eighteen years ago when we were both fresh out of Business Ad, a couple of neon-lighted idea men. Say, I know a spot for you, far less difficult than your present form of public relations — director of the Soap Manufacturers' Institute. About all that's expected is a promotional idea or two, biennial report, and annual dinner."

"But where will you say I've been the last nine years?"

"That's easy — free lancing with emphasis on direct-selling methods, the man in the street ...."

Miss Macallum was driven to clearing her throat. Even in the quiet of this office, a tension to produce, to justify the wider desk, the deeper rug.

"Mr. Phelps estimates those brochures will run about twenty-five dollars a thousand."

"Order five thousand. And get a line on scented mailing pieces —" he threw after her straight stocking seams, "Gardenia."

Soap — the place smelled of it to the sneezing point, soap in his desk drawers, on closet shelves, in merchandise displays, their bodies giving it off, a library on soap, its merchandising and manufacture. And here he sat trying to lather up ideas, surveys — how many dirty, how many clean, how many stinking, how many scented, how many bathtubs per decimal, how many cakes per tub? ... Soap for every member of the family, every part of the body ... Scrub-Yourself-Clean Week, International Soap Day ....

No job was going to ulcerate him. He undoubled his legs, beggar-lean after a year under a desk. Promotion on the hoof was prime — merchandising at the point of sale, no advertising dollar, no marketing costs, no overhead, no taxes, no personnel. A cut in income from $6,000 to a probable $3,000, but less upkeep, and a sure commodity, himself. The older he got, the better for business. Nobody could fire him — no getting out for fear he'd be kicked out.

Across the court, offices were lighted against the day, business machines, a locust hum, figures at desks, files, water coolers, all on a great elevator sinking to some sub-cellar with him, only he would make a leap for it at street level.

"Going out," he told Miss Macallum. "Don't know just when I'll be back."

"You have a three-thirty appointment with Mr. Gaynor," she reminded. "It's nearly that now."

"So?" He freed himself from the chewing-gum action of the rug for the linoleum glide out the door, did a skating turn down the marbleized hallway to wait for the liquid ruby signal — the down.

March wind was kicking a rumor of spring around, lifting veils and petticoats, sky-highing papers. Brim down, collar up, dentures pocketed, plus the look of the lost, were about all the props he needed for beggar's sport here and now. He turned in at the nearest bar, anchoring his foot to the rail.

Drinking may have walloped him into beggary, the kind of drinking that asked to get it over with, asked to be fired, asked his wife and boy to leave him, but as soon as he stopped hanging on, gave in to beggary, he had no need to drink; a successful beggar couldn't drink. You needed your wits to beg — sell, rather. He sold his people lordliness for pennies; lulled their atavism as they propitiated the stranger, perhaps the God, in their midst.

He felt his way out of the bar after he'd drunk enough courage to go back to that desk tomorrow, make somewhat of a name that his son might find if he ever came East to look him up, a name in the phone book anyway, in the directory of a big office building, in gold letters on the door, a job his son could respect .... "Dad's a public-relations man." A furnished room put him beyond reach of the boy — no phone, no name-plate — but he must make good on the job before signing any lease. That wasn't it so much as being unable to bear an apartment without Lucile and the boy, and he liked his errant room within the Broadway aureole, his shelves of books and long-playing records, a beggar's wealth secretly enjoyed, theaters, concerts, operas, bon-vivant meals but watch the waistline.

Up pitching stairs, blue with the smoke of oil burners, he unlocked a door that was churning around a bit, got rid of tie clamp, suspenders, garters, all forms of office truss, and lay back to the bong of cheap bedsprings, sobering to Beethoven's Ninth. In the lighted dusk, he turned his head toward the bureau that he kept clear of family pictures, the mirror flashing scenes of his boy as he must be now at nineteen, the two of them walking along a business street, but as he counseled on the advertising art, public-relations technique, his clothes fell away to beggary before his son. He jerked at the light cord, stopped the Beethoven short, looked in the mirror at baby-red fuzz and beggar's stubble, the flush that goes with red hair, or whisky, or both; eyes, old denim, nose, the only forceful member, and that looked as if some invisible hand were pulling him around by it. Ought to be good at begging after years of extracting money from his father. The only difference between son and father without jobs was a matter of benches, his a park bench, father's a brokerage bench in flashing view of the board and sound of the ticker tape. Had to outwit him of money meant for the margin.

Get out of here, get out fast when that dragon tail thrashes. He bent over the mirror shine of his office shoes, saw his begging shoes in the closet — so easy — slid into them without having to undo the laces, left off his tie, put on a suit that drooped like a hound's ears.

Felt good shuffling off to Pete's Tavern in easy shoes, worn thin to the pavement, the harsh and smooth of it, the dents and nodes, the slatey glide, pavements all his, diamond dusted, peanut jumbo, cracked by sycamore roots, studded with chewing gum, pock-marked, iced, puddled, cool or burning.

Nothing like Pete's spareribs. He wolfed them with a wash of good tap beer. He'd better hang on one or he'd be out on that street. One night's begging — why not? Tomorrow back to his desk. He mussed his red fuzz, pocketed his dentures, turned up his collar, and started out to streets that brightened as they darkened, the theater crowd, out to give them drama before curtain time, the beggar's tragic art, pity and terror, old as the first wanderer, current as any new disaster of which he could play victim, the actor his father wouldn't let him be, no reviews to close the show, actor's hours, sleeping late, playing nights and matinees.

March wind was blowing up a cloud of beggars along Broadway. He got out of the unprofitable rush, the poor stratagem of hurrying corners for a restaurant window near a theater where he could catch big eaters tooth-picking away the remains of blue-ribbon cuts, or edge up on the theater to make men great guys in front of their girls, at bargain rates.

Wind tore through his jacket, giving him the shivers that were good for business — a lean, hard outdoor life, this, no paunch at a desk.

A young wangler was trying to work a crowded subway entrance. "Merchants pay thousands for a good business location," he knocked off to tell him. "You can have free choice, and you set up shop where the most people make the fewest customers."

Down block, the boy did no better, mumbled and fumbled, couldn't tell likely from unlikely, his approach, a retreat. Bar courage, his own first time; even then he had only got as far as, "Which way to Fifth Avenue?" The fifty-cent piece he'd wangled in a second try had felt like a silver award in his palm for winning at a sport he kept up till he had enough to take Davie and Lucile to Jones Beach; bought him a red plastic pail and shovel, and a yellow cap with blue sailfish.

Could have started his begging career back then; went looking for work many a day, and wound up begging until in dread of Lucile finding him out, he'd gone into his drinking years, leaving job after job a jump ahead of being fired. Never secure in Lucile, the glances she threw out, the spidering fingertips; he knew she'd run off one day.

Failure was gentle as a cradle when you gave in. Once on the town, it was kind to you, even prodigal; once you stopped trying to give, they gave freely.

"Don't skulk at their heels," he told the boy. "Meet them face to face; give 'em a million-dollar story for their pennies. Quick study your people, and adapt your approach to the individual. Watch this—" He glided out to a top-hatter whose eyes were all but set in a purple veined nose. "You look like a drinking man," he said. "What would you do if you lacked just ninety-nine cents of the dollar that would purchase a quart of bourbon?"

"How long did it take you to think that one up?" said the man, paying for his laugh with a dollar bill.

The boy was behaving like a son to him, grasping his arm, saying, "Great stuff," leaping out to try the same line. "Right approach — wrong man," he counseled his pupil, and strolled over to a bookish couple with, " 'A man there was though some did count him mad, the more he cast away, the more he had.' "

That little quote from Bunyan's *Pilgrim's Progress* was good for a quarter. "Not only study your clients, but yourself," he told the boy. "What are you best at? The working man identifies himself with one type, the businessman with another. Be the gentleman beggar, the self-respecting stranger in a temporary jam. I'd say you're the rare type who can approach women, the motherly ones, I mean. In giving to you, they hope someone is being as kind to their wandering boy."

Inclining towards him, the boy was shivering in the March wind from cold, from an eagerness to learn that can send chills up your spine. "No need for acid to make pitiful sores, collodion for blindness, soap for epileptic froth, if you use your wits," he told him. "Use the advertising formula by arousing interest, attention, desire, action. Follow the laws of salesmanship right through to closing the sale with finesse for building a return clientele. A gracious closing you can use for the intelligentsia is a quotation from Cowper, 'A hand as liberal as the light of day,' or 'The truly generous is the truly wise.' In approaching this type, you might say, 'The hand that gives gathers,' or Ovid's bit of flattery, 'Giving calls for genius.' "

Could be his own son imprinting those blue eyes, and what was he teaching him? Would he say to Davie, it's like this, rheumatic fever left me with a heart that needed favoring, I was the weak kid, butt of the gang, had to develop a nimble wit, and with my old man never letting loose of a dollar, a wheedling way? Not such a bad living, Davie. Everybody's out to get something for nothing — some play Wall Street; I play every street. Years on the ragged edge of promotion pay off in this business, and the basic human appeals are all that's needed. No headstand commercials; no files the mind can't keep; no phones, no mailing pieces, no desk, no boss, no taxes. Is that what he'd tell Davie?

"Forget it," he said to the boy, "forget this ever happened. A job will turn up; they always do if you give them a chance. Maybe no one cares what you do now, but you'll meet a girl. She can't know you're a beggar; you'd never want a child of yours to know. It's a lone life. Nobody must know too much about you. As an income-tax evader you can't live up to your take or somebody'll get wise. You must appear the most wretched of men. Here take this, and don't ever let me see you again —" He put a twenty-dollar bill into his hand, and walked off. Hadn't cut his job from under him yet; had only missed a few hours at his desk; his appointment had been changed to Friday at three-thirty.

Taking it fast across Forty-seventh, he resisted prospects plump and tempting as roasting chickens, climbed his balking stairs to set his alarm clock, raised the deep-framed window and looked beyond the exfoliating brownstone sill to the Broadway borealis, the pot-o'-gold glow. Air from the river was oil-soft on the March wind, whistles of river boats searching after his son ....

Before the alarm could quite pound him awake he blocked it, opening his eyes later to the only *good morning*, sleep gone from you instead of you from sleep. He didn't know what to do with this wagging bit of forenoon — lead it on a leash to the office, or let it frisk him where it liked.

His desk would be there tomorrow. A phone call to Miss Macallum polished it up for him. He wandered toward Macy's in his free collar and easy shoes, breathed in the March air like a pony snuffling apples, put a blind boy wise that a man down the block was stealing the show by reading Braille aloud, dropped three quarters in his cup and strode on, a king of splendor, ruler of the world. His beard would spear a lot of fish as it glinted in the sun of the shopping crowd, but he must shrivel to the most abject of beggars.

A building was going up, X's chalking the windowpanes, the new customer potential — self-exorcists, salvation seekers, but-for-the-grace-of-God boys. Good old plein-air school of promotion. He'd break his Herald Square record of $53.80 in one day. Those shoppers would be a drove of mechanical toys wound to his wish.

Under Macy's overhead, he offered bargain hunters better than six per cent for cash, a saving over a check to a social agency, a transaction more personal with a sense of largess rather than duty.

He broke the monotony of their business day; made them feel like
kings so he could live like one.

Herald Square was day sport, but when the two iron men started
hammering at the evening hours,[4] he made for the forties, knocking
off a while in the park behind the Fifth Avenue library. He opened
a package of cigarettes, letting the usual two or three drop from the
pack to give some searcher-after-a-butt the sense of coming into a
fortune.

Lovers strolled under the sycamores, fooled like the expanding
buds by April in the wind. Students came along with outer arms for
school books, inner arms for each other. A girl in baby-blue fleece
was properly cuddlesome on what should be the arm of a protector.
Maybe the boy had a rheumatic heart, too — the weak one of the
gang, its dupe. The girl's eyes were all his instead of roguing after
others like Lucile's until he'd wanted to bulge them out of her head.

The girl's gloves slipped to the sidewalk when she tried to
arrange her books and handbag — downy chicks in pink angora all
but cheeping after them as the two walked on. He leaned forward
to pick them up, rubbed them like a girl's hand across his cheek,
caught up with the two, started to hand them to her when the
ineffectual way the boy tried to inch his arm along her waist, letting
her brush it off like a caterpillar, made him thrust himself beside
him. The boy went even paler than he was, huddled as if trying to
roll himself into a play-dead ball. He waggled the gloves at him.
"Want your girl's gloves? Want 'em enough to buy them back?" He
kept along with the boy's aspen steps, jogged his elbow. "Well, do
you?"

"Stop bothering us," said the boy, voice limp as a cooked onion.

The boy jerked her down the steps from the park so fast that
she almost caught her heel. "What are you trying to do, give her a
nasty fall? Is that how you look after her?" He crowded them against
the rail, nudged the boy in the ribs.

"If you don't stop annoying us, I'm going to have to speak to a
policeman."

"Fluff my nose, you're scaring me to death," he said, piping his
voice. The two ran out into the street against traffic. Halfway across
he was at the boy's elbow. "What are you trying to do? Get her

---

[4] *Two iron men.* The famous mechanical clock, constructed in 1895 and moved to
the north end of Herald Square in 1940, has a statue of Minerva over a bell, with
two cast-iron workmen who "ring" the bell each hour.

killed? Watch it, sweetheart — he won't watch for you. Never marry a man who can't take care of you."

"Won't you please let us alone?" the boy said, weak as pabulum.

"Can't handle the situation, can you? Not man enough." He followed them into the automat, around the clicking glass windows and out, ran with them toward the bus, thrusting the gloves into her pocket. "Take a tip from your beggared uncle — go find yourself the makings of a man."

The blue monoxide of the bus starting up, stenched him sober. Why had he hounded that boy, behaved like a bullying beggar, lowest of the breed? He walked fast to outdistance himself, his loose shoes clopping like bedroom slippers past office windows up and up, blue-black gleams, or gold-lighted bars for the cleaning women. He'd better be at his desk tomorrow, weight himself with it before he could ever again crouch and spring ....

Beggar's sound sleep wasn't for him, that night. He lay jittering like one of those electric signs that never get turned off on Broadway, in dark or sun. It took so long to black out that he slept through the alarm, rousing up to a clock face at a sun-streaming twelve of two.

What if he did hike over to his desk? If he stayed on the job, he'd only drink his way back to the street as usual. He phoned Miss Macallum, her voice sliding sweet as soap along the wires ... "Take care of something for me, will you? My resignation done up in impeccable Macallum style" ... "You can't mean that, Mr. Reardon. Have you forgotten your 3:30 appointment?" ... "By no means, Miss Macallum. You take over. If we ever run into each other around town, you can buy me a drink. So long, and don't let your stocking seams get crooked."

What would he do when the lovers started strolling? Taunt — jostle — bully? Shame them into giving when he could be the strange God in their midst? Committed to beggary as some to truth and right. In persecuting that boy, he had taught one man's son a lesson no father could teach him, had made him a cowering thing in front of his girl, proven that he must never let another beggar nudge, prod, insult. With any sort of stuff, the boy would come through this kind of basic training, tough and ready.

Sitting by the dry fountain of the Plaza, that evening, he leaned into the strange quiet at the heart of sound. Hansom cabs were rolling tonight. Women out walking their furs held veils and straws against breezes still chasing ahead of April.

Boy in tux, girl in tulle, were crossing the Plaza together, both a bit uncertain in evening clothes, passed so close that a spray of tulle brushed his knee. Joints cracking, he got up to put some stiffener in that young man's spine. "With what you've saved in cab fare, you can afford me the price of a drink."

The boy's arm went around the girl protectively enough. Keeping up with them, he forced them out of their straight course toward the Hotel Plaza, and into a curve around the fountain. To get away from his nudgings, the boy crowded his girl against stone that caught her tulle. As she stopped to free it, the boy threw a dollar bill at him so nervously that it spiraled away with the wind.

"Let me bully you into it, didn't you? Walk with such assurance, next time, that no one will dare. Never let another beggar throw you off your course. Now be on your way, son."

[*Prairie Schooner*, Summer 1953]

SATIN POINT

LOIS CAME DOWN OFF HER TOES and turned a close little face to Madam Vranoff. It was a Chinese puzzle of a face, skin brown-pink as a slipper orchid, with slimsy hair whipped to red lights, her willow-leaf lids a seal of secrecy over grey-blue eyes.

"How many times must I tell you, child? Relevé doesn't mean trying to stand *sur les pointes* in soft toe shoes. You could injure your feet so badly you'd never dance on point."

Between barre exercises and floor work, Lois had a full minute to arabesque in a sort of toe point. Toe shoes, satin toe shoes, what did they feel like, how did the ribbons feel; crossed about the ankles?

After class Lois went up to Madam Vranoff. "Can't I have my toe shoes now? I'm eleven, and this is my second year." Slight-boned, tall, she stood her height. "My feet are formed. You said when my feet were formed —"

"It's more than how old you are, Lois, it's how long you've studied and it's whether you're ready. Perhaps by another year —"

"Another year! Laurie Graham has her toe shoes, and she came into the class after I did."

"Laurie works: You'll find no easy way to hard-toe shoes. It takes hours, days, years of effort and ache to earn them. Even when you're first ballerina, the evening of performance, *barre* practice never stops. I've danced when the linings of my slippers were stained with blood. I danced through the last minutes of *Giselle* with an injured ankle and collapsed on stage in the midst of *Coppelia*."

Madam Vranoff walked off, leaving Lois flat-heel ugly, duck ugly, with the new class coming in, grown-ups who abused their toe shoes, let the pink satin get grimy.

Out in the reception room the dancers were sitting around, talking dance over coffee. Hair stretched tight to rosebuds; one girl was darning pink toe shoes so new they danced the light.

Miss Rogers opened her dance bag to toe shoes almost in their first pink.

"Oh, could I — would it be all right just to try them?"

"If they fit, but be careful how you stand in them or you'll injure your feet."

But no — might as well be one of Cinderella's step-sisters trying to crowd her foot into a little slipper.

"These should be about your size." The girl with the strapped ankle handed her a stretched-out pair, a pair beyond the help of benzine. She slid her feet along the worn felt to the lamb's wool. Miss Rogers showed her how to knot the ribbons, "A bow could come undone and trip you."

Just as she was about to stand *sur les pointes*, Madam Vranoff clapped her hands sharp as a snapped branch. "Off — take them off this instant. You haven't earned them. Do you hear?" Madam Vranoff's neck splotched purple. "You haven't earned them, you haven't earned them."

With Madam Vranoff standing over her as she undid the knot, she was like a soldier stripped of buttons and epaulets. She walked toward the elevator to pass the Davlin studios where the dancers were always stretching and toe pointing out into the corridor. Most everyone in toe shoes, cared-for toe shoes.

She crossed Fifty-seventh Street in a satin-soft breeze for September, looked in all the shop windows with dance themes in honor of The Royal Ballet here on a visit from England. *Swan Lake* tonight, Fonteyn dancing. Mama had sent for tickets back in March. She stood before a wardrobe trunk open to costumes from the Rose Adagio, Bluebird *pas de deux*, a little plate skirt from the last act of *Sylvia*. Toe shoes in another window were gathered to a bouquet of colors, the ribbons hanging down to reds, blues, pinks, greens. Oh, she could gather up an armful.

When she went to the ballet that night Lois let out her hair rrom the tight-wound braids Madam Vranoff made her wear in class. Coming down the aisle of the Met she could see out the side of her lids — *lotus lids*, her teacher had called them — very ballerina — could see people looking at her, wondering, the set to her head, the walk, wondering was she a dancer. Sixth row seats, side aisle, but sixth row. *That's why I keep my office job*, mama told her, *to give you the advantages we couldn't afford otherwise. I want your talents developed to the full.*

"Mama — mama — look underneath the curtain!" — toe shoes reflected on a blue lake of light. She looked down at the pair of toe shoes on the book cover of the ballet book, toe shoes on very point, the long instep, ribbons crossed about the ankles, pink point toe shoes, satin point, jewel point. The world should stop just here on toe point.

"I want to change teachers," she told her mother at intermission.

"Change teachers!" Mama exclaimed. "Why I thought you could hardly believe your good fortune to be studying with Madam Vranoff."

"Just because she was a great dancer doesn't mean she can teach. She frightens me."

Curtain going up again, the golden curtain, its brocade sliding up in luxury folds. Toes, the pebbled sound of all the toes. Mists of tulle, the falling away of arms like a wave, the surfing toe points.

Fonteyn — Fonteyn in her swan sadness. Lois felt herself reddening in the audience dark for wanting the toe shoes so much. Cymbals, the clap of Madam Vranoff's hands — *Off* — *take them off — you haven't earned them, you haven't earned them!*

"I'm too nervous with Madam Vranoff. In a *ronde de jambe* she even hit my leg back where it was supposed to go."

Mama touched her forehead in that lost memo way. "I don't know, Lois. Maybe she's just trying to wake you up. I wonder why you ever fancied anything as strenuous as ballet."

"And she plays favorites. I never get much of her time." Curtain up and away to satin point. Oh those shoes in the Neapolitan dance — the green-green of peacocks.

Black points for Odile. Fonteyn's feather steps, her *fouettées* — thirty, thirty-one; thirty-two, thirty-three, thirty-four — Oh! Everybody stopped breathing at the *arabesques*.

"I want to study at the Davlin studio, Mother," head spinning with points like sea glitter.

"Why haven't you mentioned this studio till now? I'd think if—"

"I wasn't ready before. Now I'm ready."

"Well, if you'd be happier — work better."

"Oh I knew it — I knew you would —" Hugged so tight the comb nearly fell out of Mama's hair. "I'll have my toe shoes in no time — my pink satin toe shoes."

With Mama worked around to the new studio, she tried to talk Madam Davlin into advancing her to a class where she would wear hard shoes part of the time, but her teacher smiled her into the beginners' class, "Only for a while — until you learn our ways."

After holding off into February, she asked Madam Davlin, "May I have my toe shoes now?"

"You're not ready yet, dear. You need to work much harder. Besides, even our advanced students seldom wear them, they cover up sloppy toe work, make you think you're doing better than you are —"

"If I had my toe shoes I'd work harder."

"They're something to look forward to — rather like a first graduation."

Mama bent over her bed that night looking very much like a lilac fairy. "How is the dancing coming?"

I'm ready for toe shoes. The lie she almost told her mother was black in the dark — black as Odile.

An eye, next day, a mascaraed eye stared at her from the cover of a fashion magazine on all the news stands, stared through to the lie. All during Church School, she could see the eye.

Monday after class she went to the phone booth on the corner, "Mama, I know I shouldn't be disturbing you during business hours, but this is important, I'm — I'm ready for toe shoes. Can we get them right now?"

"I don't see how I can leave the office early, Lois."

"Oh please— just this once, this special once —"

"Well, all right — this special once."

The eye, the mascara'd eye followed her to the ballet shop, winked her up the steps with her mother, past painted walls to pink satin ribbons unwinding to toe shoes. Opened the door to photographed murals of dancers caught and held forever in *developpé, battierie, arabesque.*

"We would like to see toe shoes," Mama told the salesgirl.

"Hard toe, Mama."

"Yes, hard toe. In what color, do you think, Lois? Pink?"

"And green — do you have a peacock green? Oh, and red, and—"

"Softly — softly — let's start with the pink, although black might be more —"

"Oh no — pink."

The salesgirl took them out of the tissue too scrabbly fast for such pink perfection, held them just like any shoes. They fitted first time — hers. She stroked the satin along her cheek, the hard soft.

"And the black — don't you think I should have the black to keep these nicer?"

"I'm afraid our budget can't take two pairs right now — maybe later —"

"But you said that's what you're keeping your job for, so I can have extras. They're so fragile, Mother. Dancers wear out three and four in one night's performance."

"Your feet are growing — you're —"

"Oh, I can't choose — not between Odette and Odile."

The salesgirl wanted to send them. "No — oh no —" She carried them home with her — each in its special box — the black and the pink. Next, the red — the green.

While Mama stitched the black satin ribbons just where they should be for her ankles, she slid her feet into the pink ones already sewn, slid through to the lamb's wool, pushed against the hardness. Steadying herself against the piano, she rose to the delicious little hurt of *sur les pointes*, stood, just stood, on point — the jewel-drop moment.

Clap, the clap of Madam Vranoff's hands, she heard it in the drop of the piano rack — *haven't earned them — you haven't earned them.* She put *Swan Lake* on the phonograph, turned it up so loud her Mother held her ears; turned it softer, stood as long as she could balance on satin point to the Odette theme, down on them, up on them.

Mama took one last stitch, broke thread, and handed her the black satin. She came off toes beginning to ache, unwound the satin ribbons, slipped off the Odette shoes to try the Odile, hugged them both to her, the ribbons hanging down bouquet, hugged them so hard they hurt.

SMASHEROO

AN ACROBAT of a March wind tossing sunlight about, whipping him into shape to walk in on that music publisher and say, *Look here, what are you doing to put my song across? It's time I had something to show for my two hundred and fifty smackers.*

First he'd peddle his new song. Not often between jobs like this ... he must do months in a day. Ruthie would call the tune, she'd name off the kids' needs if she knew he wasn't blistering his heels around personnel departments and employment agencies in the morning hours, but this lion wind pushed him right on past, turned him in at 1657. Song in it somewhere ... a lion up Broadway, lion on the loose ... lion, lion, who's a-cryin'?

The elevator tight with people protecting envelopes like perishables. "Lousy machines," some man was saying, "don't give your song a chance."

What floor? One's as good as another. Floors of doors .... A tin-pan-alley piano pulled him off at the sixth, pied-pipered him to a door marked *Arranging Room*, partly open to a beat-up grand in old drawing-room green and gilt. A kid standin' above the arranger, blatted *luv-lu-uv-lu-u-u-uv* like that one word was all you needed to make 'em cry hit. A hit had to do more than blah love, it had to tell a story, and you didn't come in with lead notes expectin' the arranger to take over; then it wasn't your song.

Everything about his songs was his own, lyrics, melody, chord progressions. He could do everything but sing 'em, put 'em across. The few rush times he'd stuck his flat nose and flap ears out of the stock room of fancy department stores to sell, the customers didn't even take him for a salesman.

With his slob features, he still wanted after the long-legged girls he passed on the street . . . passed on the street but never did meet, a song maybe .... They looked right over his head, those long steppers with their high proud lines, but if he had a crackle of green in his pocket and a hit song for them to sing ... No, he was more comfortable with his Ruthie, a pineapple chunk, but cute like his song said, *My Ruthie's no beaut but she sure is cute.*

Wham, it hit you walkin' into this waiting room, all their top tunes framed round the wall, the big-money babies, the smasheroos.

His up there ... seeable is believable ... someday maybe ... You didn't have to be no genius in this business, it could be you.

Beer-bold, he said to the receptionist, "Tell your boss I have a song hit for him."

"Have you an appointment?"

"No, but I'll wait — "

"You'll have a long one. He's in Hollywood."

"Then I'll settle for whoever's hearin' hits today. This won't keep."

"Mr. Garvin attends to all that personally. Of course if you care to leave a copy of the song or a recording."

"Do I look that dumb?"

A bigger publisher down the hall, door after door all theirs, hits opening out like fans on the reception-room walls.

"Anybody around to hear my new song?"

"Mr. Reese and Mr. Miesner are both out of town," said the receptionist. "Come back in May."

Come back in May and then they'll say, No, no, come back in June, but that's too soon .... "By that time they'll be whistlin' my song in the streets."

"Mr. Reese and Mr. Miesner are prepared to take that chance."

Not looking for songs, these publishers, only for the one song, top hit. Why not work on the little publishers after the hit to make them big? He'd hang onto his good nature by saving the gyp what had his two fifty for last, the showdown. Still paying the loan company and they hadn't promoted his song with a single disk jockey or band or singer.

Schaaf's Music Corporation ... small enough to give him a hearing. He waited for the receptionist to wipe the lipstick off her teeth. "I've a song to run through for the boss."

"If you'll leave a copy with me, I'll see that —"

"Oh, no, I don't leave nothin.' I'll wait."

She riffled her pleats into the inner office. A man with brief case bursting its zipper came in humming a tune bad enough to be his own.

"Sorry" ... receptionist in unsorry tones ...

"Mr. Eckle is tied up. Try us in another three weeks."

"But I'll have a nine-to-five job by then. Can't he hear this one song?"

"Sorry that's the best he can do. Why not leave us a recording if you have one?"

"I'm sick of that routine. Nothin' ever comes of it. I got just the one record with me, and this one day to play it in. It's his last chance to get himself a hit."

"Sorry."

Still whistling his song flop, goon tune got her go ahead ... You need time to go round and around till you're known. He took to the stairs, humming his own song. The man on the landing could be a publisher, could say, *What's that you're humming? I know a hit when I hear one.* ... Chance had a lot to do with it in the song-writing business, grabbing a wrong overcoat, or sitting in the right barber chair. A popular-song writer is no one-of-a-kind genius, no Brahms, Schumann, Schubert. Thousands of songs could be hits . . . yours had to be heard, promoted. Felt like shaking this big rich building by the throat, making it listen.

A couple of girls, their song envelopes clutched limp at the edges, were coming up the stairs to his down. "You look battered," said the first shortie; "don't let those publisher boys catch you down beat."

"Up and down we go" ... tweedlededum.

"We never take no"... tweedlededee.

"Pay a flop no mind, your next can be a hit. We start first thing every morning and trudge from floor to floor. You can't wear those publishers down without wearing down your heels. No song is so much better it's worth publishing over yours. In this racket, one slob's as good as another. Writing a song is a breeze; it's the marketing that takes all your time and wits."

"Sure, that's all right if you don't have to work for a livin.' See you in wax — "

Downbeat to the street ... downbeat to the street ... street ... street ...Footfalls undertoned the traffic noise, his own steps in shoes Ruthie shined for job hunting. Stern's department store only a couple of blocks, he ought to put in his application at the personnel office, it could take weeks for an opening. He was always having to do it over again, just as he would work up to head of stock he would make some fool mistake or tell somebody off and he'd be out. *Sometimes I think you get yourself fired on purpose,* Ruthie would rag

him, *so you can run around tin-pan-alley or sit on a park bench dreamin'
up songs when you should be job hunting.*

"Aren't my songs just as good as the ones you listen to every day
on TV and radio — maybe better? You sing my songs about the
house, don't you, just like everybody could be singing 'em? It only
takes one hit like Billy Hill's *The Last Round Up.*"

Sixty dollars a week is better than maybe a million, she'd say.

Should get over to Stern's to give him something to talk to Ruth
about, but they might railroad him into an immediate job the way
Gimbel's had just when he needed time to market a new song.
Maybe he wouldn't have wasted two fifty on a phony publisher-
promoter if he could have gone the rounds.

Record shops loud-speakered song hits no better than his ... *Let
me gao, let me gao, let me gao lu-u-ver* ... never moved off the shelves
when it was called *Let me go devil* ... some publisher really worked
on it .... His own publisher a candy apple over the phone ... this time
he'd surprise Mr. Mertz by appearing in person ... *Let me gao, let me
gao* ... that flat style of singing, that *pi-ie* in the *ska-y*, made every
song sound phony. If he ever got to be somebody, they would have
to change their style or they couldn't sing his songs ... he'd change
tin-pan alley to folk alley . . . not folk-and-don't-know-it, writing
down to folk, but real folksongs.

Clouds gone to wind, blue sailing ... a day to sail a song ship.
He crossed to Duffy Square, humming his new song too low for
anyone to steal ... pigeons all but cooing it, nice little contralto
pigeons, better than those disc birds — the jitter singers, hog callers,
heart's blooders ... a lot of them birds couldn't exist without
amplifiers, nature never meant 'em to be singers.

What about his own self? Was he ever meant to write songs? No
prodigy like most musical people he'd read about. A kid in that
gosh-awful street of orange brick in Queens against another street
of orange brick and another street of orange brick. He would go
can-kicking through a vacant lot with sooty sunflowers tall as him,
stop to look across the river to the sky-reachin' buildings, and songs
would come crowdin', only he didn't have no Mozart father to teach
him how to set 'em down. They just went out to the air.

The songs he could write if he knew more about composition.
Tried to study out them fancy books on harmony and counterpoint
by himself, but they was worse than algebra. The home-study course

in chord progression helped, and the lightning arranger, but it was like gangsters trying to get to the top fast and shaky.

His very piano he only came by because it was left behind in the apartment building ... couldn't afford the repairs and it was too far gone for a piano tuner. The best place for his tunes was still his head, but if they like your tune, an arranger can always fix it up, you don't need long years of training to turn out a hit.

"Folk" to the tin-panners meant hillbilly, and they production-lined 'em in clouds of monoxide. For folk art, you should be folk, live folk, want to do something about folk, sing the song of the little guy beatin' his brains out, never gettin' nowhere, never havin' nothin' to show for his sweat. What he saw in museums said that everyday things could be beautiful if real folk made 'em whole.

What would it be like to be village folk, a fisherman in a stocking cap on the isle of Capri, makin' up fishing songs as he mended his net? ... now it was the world or no go. No wonder you read in the paper about some little guy shootin' through the streets or firin' at a speeding train ... hear us, know we exist.

Wouldn't it be great if he could teach the pigeons his song, and they would fly around singing it until everyone in the streets caught it up, asked for it in the music shops, and that music publisher would have to pull thousands of copies off the presses, wax thousands more, name bands playing, top singers singing?

Come, get a move on, a song to peddle, a score to settle, and precious little time. He turned in at the building where his publisher had his office. He would try one or two more outfits before the showdown.

Grubby little offices like the sunflower lot, livings hard come by, his new song might lift one of them out of it.

Not even a receptionist in this office. A man in shirt sleeves, "What can I do you for — do for you?"

"I have a song —"

"Who hasn't? Not today, we're in the process of reorganization."

"A spin of the disc can change your luck."

"Trouble is, we spin too many discs."

He hotfooted it to those wise guys while they were still in business. The joint even looked shady, ready to burn the books and records and get out ... not set up to receive people, a mail-order air ... they ought to be living it up with all the money they took in when they should be laying it out, but the furniture appeared second, third, fifth hand, everything a jump ahead of receivership.

Chinless, her hair tangled horsetail, the girl never looked up from the switchboard where she was mailing out false hopes for your money. By phone, by mail, safe away from a punch in the nose.

"Tell Mr. Mertz I'm here, Miss. The name's Larrabee, Howard Larrabee."

"What is it in reference to?" ... crisp like her blouse wasn't.

"My song it's in reference to. You're supposed to be promoting it, remember? You have two hundred and fifty of my smackers what says so."

"Don't take it out on me, genius. I only fold and mail."

"Then show me in to Mr. Mertz."

"Mr. Mertz is not with us anymore."

"Who's in Mr. Mertz's shoes?"

"No one — they're all out."

"I'll wait."

"Out of town."

"I wait."

Pigeons cooing on the ledge ... he hummed pigeon-low, the song they had shelved. Did she catch it, lilt it, like the movies where workmen stopped workin', passersby walkin', no, she kept on folding those phony announcements.

All out, eh? Somebody knockin' about in there. He bypassed horsetail, tempted to pull out her shirttail all the way.

Another chinless inside, double chinless, at his thermos coffee and crullers. Looked rat-cornered, but so did the most innocent folk surprised at a lone meal. "I'm Larrabee — Howard Larrabee, one of your song writers."

"Nice to meet you in person, Mr. Larrabee."

"I gave you two hundred and fifty dollars to publish a song of mine, and I want to know what you're doing to promote — "

"We're working on it. Your song is promising, most promising. However, if all our song writers dropped in on us, we'd never get time to promote their songs. Now would we? This is a cooperative enterprise. We try to do so much for so many."

"Well, this one-of-the-many wants a face-to-face accounting."

"Like I said, we're working on it. Just the other day we had a singer interested —"

"I've a right to know how you're spendin' my two fifty."

"You have no idea of the expense involved. Your money would nowhere near cover it if this wasn't a cooperative enterprise with many new song writers pooling their resources. Printing costs are out of sight, and we pay one of the best autographers in the business, and an arranger for the professional touch, or any last-minute changes to suit a singer's style. Besides we have to wine and dine our prospects."

"Show me the files — show me where my song's been, who's interested —"

"We can't keep a record on every contact. Folks come in and out of here all day long searching for new songs."

"So I see."

"Like all new song writers, you're too impatient. It takes time and —"

" —a bigger staff. I know, I work for a livin'. Suppose you show me the five hundred copies you said you printed."

"Certainly."

Almost felt sorry for the goon as he haunched to the file drawer, for all the passing notes Broadway could strike out and never miss. All so beat up around the song buildings, the unfolk alley tryin' for the one little disc that would set the globe spinning with a song. Just a little grubber, no big villain to take a poke at.

"See, they're all here, ready to push when the time" ... the time, never the time ... all here with their sleazy pea-green covers buttercupped and butterflied ... poor autographing ... notes should be black caps, mad caps, so lively they made you want to sing. He scooped up as many of his songs as he could hold. "You can't do that. Put them back."

"Sure can. I paid my fortune."

"What do you expect us to do? We can't cram your song down their throats. It's no *Cry*."

Hanging onto his songs, he slammed out of that gyp joint and down the stairs ... No, not out to the street yet, not one of the crowd, footfalls undertoning the traffic noise.

He climbed back up the stairs past gyp doors, closed doors, up five flights to the roof.

A trumpeting day large enough to put a world of songs across ... his songs.

Big empty sign, almost bigger than the roof, big like the sign he'd seen in a movie, the pursued in lone splendor up here, the gasping crowd far below. Lone pigeon on a cornice across the way ... bird shadow swifting across a billboard ... felt like Jupiter up here.

He leaned over the parapet to Broadway ... "and in their hands they shall bear thee up lest thou dash thy foot against a stone" ... the line in the Bible he most wanted to believe, that, and about the hairs of your head bein' numbered.

Stone buildings scrubbed in March wind, towering for the street crawl. Six men across, worked on inches of sign to paint the face bigger than life, the global movie star ... star body of last week's premiere coming down piece by piece in pulleyed sections.

Shots from a rifle range ... any minute they could be real shots from the gun of some little Joe bustin' loose from the crawl crowd.

Broadway lights, a tic on the face of day ... clouds no more than paper wisps making the sky look all the more cloudless ... Lone gull ... no, a bit of street paper flying high. He let a song sail out on the wind. It fell under car wheels, hopped a little ways like a hurt bird, fell back under more wheels, was dragged out of sight.

Sailed another ... it went down wind to the sidewalk ... A man stooped to read what it said, someone else picked it up, let it fall from his hand to the trampling crowd. He let go another ... it glanced off a woman's hat, her little girl ran to pick it up, rolled it to a tooting horn, a ball bat to strike parking signs.

Two more down wind ... one landed on the hood of a car, the other crossed to Duffy Square, startling the pigeons to flight. He let go a bunch close to the building. People picked them up, looked them over, maybe humming, whistling. Others were looking up to see where they came from. He let go another bunch and another, Broadway blowing white with his songs, passerby picking them up, perhaps to take home, play, sing, he was getting past the tin alley curtain to folk.

Footsteps crunching the graveled roof ... a song publisher maybe ... wackier things happened in this business. A cop.

"Just what d'ya think you're doing?"

"Givin' the folks down there a great little song."

"You're littering, that's what you're doing" ... ketchup-faced cop so sure with his stick ... "Ya better come along with me."

"What for? I was only tryin' to put my song across. You don't arrest big advertisers for litterin' with their balloons and plane scatterings and street handouts. Why me?"

Thick knuckled, he took out his pad and started makin' out a ticket like in a traffic violation.

"Give a guy a break. I didn't know I was goin' against the law. I won't do it no more. I'm outa work, can't pay no fine."

"Ya should've thought of that before you violated the sanitation code." Fat knuckles just kept on writin'. Below they were still bending down to pick up his songs.

"Please, Mister, let me off with a warning this once. You know how it is. I got kids, three of 'em."

"Don'cha know you could've caused a traffic accident if one of them sheets had hit a windshield and obscured the driver's view?"

"Guess I didn't think, I was so excited over my song. Take a look at it, you'll see it's a hit."

"Can't carry a tune."

"Well, listen —" He started to hum it through.

"All right, all right, goon, get down off this roof. I'll let you off with a warnin', this time."

Not even a four-star crime, not worth pullin' him in. He went down into the street, the left-over songs blowin' against folk's legs, trampled, soiled, one or two still reached for, but mostly blowing all around, litter, like the cop said . . . *blowin' all around, never touchin' ground* . . . a song in it somewhere.

[Prairie Schooner, Spring 1956]

HANDSHAKE

THIS IS THE WAY we shake your hand, shake your hand, shake your hand ... Mr. Rawlins all but spelled with his handshake ... "Don't let this thing ruin you. It could, you know." Mrs. Lindsey laced fingers ... "They don't know what they're doing. Wherever will we find another such minister?"

Miss Simms fluttered his hand like a pigeon trying to eat out of it. She had made the air white with petitions when even the church head who had sponsored him turned him back on the board. *Warned you not to stress social action in that parish, and now with the domestic complications, I can't cram you down their throats.*

Simple, the charges. "If he can't hold his own home together, how can he preach to us of family life?" And the fister to those pointing out that it was no divorce, only a separation after they had seen their son through his growing years. "We have reason to believe he's something of a Red."

The Parish Hall would be echoing empty with only the few faithful at this farewell reception, but the neck-stretchers crowded it in curiosity as they never did in fellowship. Fellowship, humanity, ingathering, outreach — all such familiar words were hardening into gems to turn coldly in the hand.

Music marching through his mind, marching them up for their handshake to the tune of his inner ear, Elgar's *Pomp and Circumstance*. "You're no real Red, I keep telling them" ... Mr. Bogert's golf grip ... "that being the case, McCarthy could have you up on charges."

Arm twists of good church people. They meant to hurt, not meaning to, their rancors driving up through the tactless remark. His momentary wryness over a rash of board members must not cloud him against all humans ... "no question about it, you're a victim of your wife" ... Mrs. Bogert paddycaked his hand in both hers.

To the throat-clearing point that used to get on Edith's nerves, his irritation all gone to throat. This room-choke weed, he'd have to cut a path through to the April sunlight that hung about like a stray at a door opening less and less. The long table lit by pink candles that waxed the body heat, a feast for his farewell, such as he wanted the pinch-pennies to spread for the Junior Highs. Red, for working to strengthen their youth program, build a Youth Center open to all; Red, for carrying Visitation Evangelism to the unchurched along the city's waterfront; Red, for trying to start a rehabilitation program for displaced persons; Red, for any hint of social action that could be interpreted by these business execs as a possible pressure group when they would outright lobby for the least profit.

Seven years ago, walking up the path to this Church above the Hudson, marigolds renewing their suns against the grey stone, he had thought — had thought — How had he thought? His parish, his people, the kind of conservatives he had grown up with, were neglected by the zealous for work with the underprivileged, but how better help the underprivileged than by jogging the privileged out of their lethargy? The *haves*, the most neglected group, the true charity cases of the spirit.

In his student pastorates he had been too storming, but he had learned to temporize or he wouldn't have lasted these seven years.

"Estimable sermon," the elderly Mr. Olcott mistaking the occasion of the handshake.

"It's not Sunday," shouted his niece. "Mr. Laurent doesn't preach his final sermon until Sunday. This is a farewell party — farewell party. He's leaving us, you know — leaving us —"

His very looks had ill-eased them when he first took the pulpit—"hair an uncombed halo," his secretary had put it, "rather the way I'd pictured John the Baptist, a look more like a listening, your head lifted, inclined, as if you were hearing wonderful things for us that would change our lives then and there." Not since his student pastorates had he spoken *truth*. His words modified for them, by them, tenderized to Sunday dinner sermons.

The Corliss sisters, tentacling words and fingers, their scent inking around him. His skin would split if he didn't get out into the day. "Your skin's stretched so tight you look like a deaths-head under that lamp," Edith had thrown across to him from the couch where she puffed, soft as a cold pigeon. Saw himself deaths-head lately, his eyes burning so deep in their sockets that it took a long mirror look to see whether they still burned or were just skull holes.

Marching, marching to the Elgar tune of his inner ear, tune too grand for McCarthy times, small-town gossip making good out in the big world, TV, newspapers, nation's committee rooms. Just like people too self-conscious to be seen in anything so outmoded, intolerance raged back into fashion. McCarthiettes could wear what they were proudly, as *Peel Me, I'm Chocolate.* Ends could justify means again, inquisitors could call themselves investigating committees, and whatever it is you don't like, call it *Red.*

Board trouble had started when it ousted the choirmaster for Red tendencies, when he put a DP[5] in as soloist over a local bleater, and defended Gieseking[6], Shostakovich[7], even Robeson[8].

"You're loyal, I tell everyone, absolutely loyal," Mrs. Carr's conviction more in her words than her handshake.

"A divorce — separation, I mean — takes two, I contend," said the wife of one of the board members who had leaned his way, "but in this case, no, she just wasn't up to being a minister's wife. Mind, I don't think any the less of her. I wouldn't be up to it myself. My husband has some sort of virus or he'd be here saying the same thing."

At the moment he favored the faithless who gave him no farewell and came to none. Heads turning at a door scuff that could be Edith crashing the party. Rumors had her a lone drinker when she was just lone, had him driving her to it with his passion for his secretary, poor, lone, faithful Andrews.

Edith, a pale lovely moonstone in her father's parsonage, spinning dreams fine as her hair, letting down ropes of the pale moon stuff for a lover to climb. If he had a fire that attracted her, she complained it was only for the Gospel. Her father's student, he had married the daughter as if she were his way of life, as if his wisdom were contained in her; had taken her from her father's parsonage to his with her notion of fashion-magazine life. Promise

<hr>

[5] *DP.* Displaced person, i.e., someone who had been a war refugee after World War II.

[6] *Gieseking.* Concert pianist Walter Gieseking was accused of being a Nazi sympathizer.

[7] *Shostakovich.* Soviet composer Dimitri Shostakovich, ironically considered an apologist for Soviet communism while he was actually one of its tormented victims.

[8] *Paul Robeson.* African-American singer and actor, an activist who had visited Soviet Russia.

— not much left but the figure of the young man of promise, the tried juvenile, white-blonded, spring-arched.

Must get out of here, walk off the shell emptiness of Elgar. Andrews ready to head him off at the April door, just as she had reasoned him to the back of the Church, Sunday, to shake the hands that were against him.

No, he would neither blurt nor bolt, he would stand to the last saliva spray.

Andrews did cut the last knots for him with a reminder of letters that must get out tonight, the final sermon to prepare. He crossed the lawn to the parsonage in a sunset tinge of red lilacs, marigolds still green in their buds.

Most of their things in storage, Edith wanting reminders no more than he did. The places where the pictures had been, clean as new whittled wood. His books stood in crates ready to be shipped to a student room on the sabbatical the Board had presented to him with a feeling of Christian dismissal.

His desk, set like a lone place at table, demanded a decent last sermon. He turned on his lamp against the sunset. A hairpin bent pale gold between the floor boards. His thoughts slithered away from what he hadn't been to Edith as her hair from her pins. How could he think through a sermon when he no longer thought through for himself?

He pocketed a scratch pad and pencil, and started toward the Hudson to walk a sermon under the red-scarred heavens. He raged along to the thrust of the salt tide up the river. Red rocks glowed through the misting green as if in molten remembrance of ancient upheaval. His text — what would it be? Hate had closed the book to him, hate breaking out like fevered boils. His throat still bothered him. Nobody would believe it if he came down with another attack of laryngitis before the last sermon.

On the outs with God's people, same as being on the outs with God, but he only raged against those about the board, their mouths tight-drawn purse strings as they opposed every coat of paint, every bit of carpentry.

In the bat-flying light he could no more pick sermon words out of the air than bats' wings. Couldn't outmarch Elgar. Easier to love the underdog, more tangible to work with the poor, yet *have-nots* nothing but potential *haves*. All that slobbering to better them that they in turn can oppress, no better by virtue of being underprivileged.

Admit it. You don't like people — a minister, and you don't like people.

Can no longer put it off on Edith, her aloofness, her way of seeing through everyone that overlooks any good.

Then why had he entered the ministry? People, loved people, dedicated himself to just such spiritually underprivileged as the board, had to crack through to the abusers of power, the *have* hardened. But collectively — people, not persons, groups, not individuals, as he might shape them, not as they are. The great commandment deceptively simple, *Thou shalt love thy neighbor as thyself*. Easier to scale a glass mountain, drain the sea.

His very choice of the ministry involved his deep-down dislike of people as individuals. In a minister relationship with people, he thought he would be seeing them at their Sunday best, walking among them in love and honor.

Exhausted wrestling with his angel of self-knowing ... He stretched out on old leaves and new green shoots, the ground damp enough from winter to make him lose his voice, but a hand had been lifted from his throat. No longer out of sorts with spring as he had been for some seasons, the Hudson, cold green metal, birdcalls, the grating of chalk across a blackboard ... now willow garlands, a green woven basket around him in the bulrushes of blue-green light ... "Ye must be born again" ... not since student pastorates, this revelation. A tongue of fire in the days before plush pews. What would he say to them Sunday from the pulpit when he should be down among them?

A light in the parsonage marigolding out to the stone sill. Andrews, Miss Simms, the Keeblers, waiting for him, the fragrance of a coffee welcome, sandwiches set out on the card table. Andy had even disheveled his desk a bit to take away the bare waiting for final words.

"We've been so worried about you back here." Miss Simms overfilled his cup. "Oh, dear me, now there's no room for the cream. If you hadn't gone so hard and fast on those long legs of yours we would have walked with you —"

A new ease with them now that he had faced himself. "Can't speak another word to anyone. I'll have one sip of this good coffee and go on upstairs."

The ones who had watched with him, their heads bent to the lamp-light, he loved them. Loving beyond likes and dislikes, catching up annoyances like beach drift in surf. As one of them, liking, disliking, he could admit their motives. The Keeblers rallied to him only because they had been snubbed by certain members of the board; he could admit that Miss Simms was tedious, that Andy got on his nerves sometimes, without darking over his love in perfectionist self-conflict. Easier to love your neighbor when you stop working at it.

In the days left to him he walked farther up the Hudson, higher into the hills. If he could just reach up his arm and be handed his sermon on a tablet of stone, but he no longer sought to be Moses burning the golden calf, turning sword against sword. It was *we*, not *you*. He was getting his voice back; he preached to the red rocks, the flowering trees, the hills in change everlasting.

Downtown after one of these walks he ran into Mr. Hofstader, shut face against him, saw him as for the first time, saw deep into his death fear. No longer stumbling over self as he walked along a street of faces, he could see through to their being, see them in God's time, a thousand years as a watch in the night.

Sunday he started to mount the pulpit, but came back down to stand among them. Andrews was straining her hands, reaching them out like a mother fearful of her child's first steps.

"Being a Christian is not so easy as we think. It can be summed in a sentence, *Love one another*. Keep this commandment and you keep all the rest. But do you approach it? Do I?" ... voice of his first days, student voice ... could feel them as one in the Word ... "You may think we've made a poor job of this commandment as minister and board, a commandment still to be reached, surely; but it can be if we go beyond differences to God's love that catches up our likes and dislikes in a love for all creation." ... In the intimacy of the low burning lights, he was getting through to them ... if they felt, lived just one sermon, it bloomed the seven years.

" 'Love thy neighbor as thyself.' You needn't like everything about your neighbor any more than you like everything about yourself. Love is in God. It can start with looking around you, seeing

<124>

everything as for the first time, the many greens of early spring, bird in flight, the markings of a turtle; it can start with a listening, the way the wind takes different voice in maples, willows, poplars, reeds, and go on to loving all creation, and your neighbor ..."

Silence of true listening. Andy came up to him, eyes tear-jeweled ... some still sat in their pews making no move to go, not speaking, as after music ... Mrs. Henderson crying ... a few heads still bowed in prayer. He went to the front of the church for the first handshake.

[*Prairie Schooner*, Winter 1955]

SAPPHIRA SITTER

THE SIAMESE SAT tall on her radiator cushion as the Brandts interviewed me for the job of cat sitter. Her pedigree paper unrolled right back to the court of Siam, her royal ancestry written in Manchu Bells, Ramu Firsts, Seconds, Thirds, her own name, Princess Sapphira.

"Your nails," said Mrs. Brandt, "you'll have to clip them for Sapphira's safety."

"Why not clip *her* claws; they're wicked."

"Never, they're her beauty and her defense."

"Mine too. I get occasional calls to model my hands."

"No smoking," said Mr. Brandt. "It bothers her."

"A dancer rarely smokes." Sapphira's smell test could lose me the job, with the sweating I'd just done at the *barre*. Her sapphire stare had me checking my blouse front for missing buttons. Ballet students can't all have scholarships or work around the studio; dancers have sprung their arches waiting on table or standing at a sales counter, and on this fur-lined job, you sit.

"A frosty night," said Mrs. Brandt stretching her plump arms to get down satin quilt, pillow, yellow silk pajamas from Sapphira's closet. "Her bed is radiant heated, you don't have to plug anything in."

Just what I needed in a furnished room, too high for the heat to be any more than a noise in the pipes, but this place sealed in cat.

"No windows up at any time," said Mr. Brandt looking like a chlorined carp up for oxygen. "She's defenseless against the common cold. Kindly don't report for work if you feel yourself coming down with one. Being sixteen stories above the park is another reason for securing the windows."

Handing me a typed instruction sheet, they went out the door in overcoat and Persian sprilled with her two-toned hairs. A duty for every interval. No cat sitter — cat currier and scurrier. Brush fur, starting at head and working gently down to tip of tail. Bathe eyes in boric acid. Serve all food and drink at room temperature. Beat egg into cup of milk. Broil sirloin rare, mash a clove of garlic in with peas.

Under her gem-cut stare, my blues paled. Her royal mask turned me into a sweat-faced mutt. Her two tones modulating from cream to sable coarsened my carrot. But the tail, I did a *pas de chat* at the tail, crooked, crumpled, ignominious.

Sapphira's scrapbook bulged with press clippings when mine wasn't so much as started. She had won all available ribbons and prizes. A crooked tail was a show point for a Siamese. Sapphira paid my wages out of her own fur pocket. A successful model, she was photographed with everything from jewels to fountain pens to suggest like perfection in the product; had sat for painters and sculptors; been a stage cat when I hadn't so much as danced on as a snowflake.

"Here punkins, here some punkins —" As I reached down to pet her expensive fur, I received the royal bite, for which she got a ballerina's kick. Her voice, her banshee voice — tail, a sceptre passing angry sentence.

Between brushings and vitamin feedings, both of which I could use, I boned up on the proper respect for *cat*, worshipped as Mau, Goddess in ancient Egypt, trained by Pharaohs to hunt in packs like dogs, to guard the palace against breakers and enterers. Fire-eyed, they leapt hell-spitting on the backs of altar thieves. Egyptian law demanded that a man mourn a dead cat by shaving his eyebrows. Death was the sentence for killing a cat. A cat cult took such hold of the *Fraus* during the Middle Ages that they behaved like cats in the full of the moon, which put the Vatican in the position of burning witches and dooming your kind to death. Still you persisted until you got a reputation for nine lives. With mice about, you were kept in secret, rumored as Goblins who catch mice and drink saucers of milk left on door stones. Rodents came into such power that you had to be restored openly to kill the rats that spread the plague, catch the mice that foul the grain, keep millers prosperous, towns settled, and now you're the breadwinner.

The temple bell around Sapphira's neck was the only coolness in this cat sty. I raised the bathroom window a slit, and using the towel rack for a barre, did my *pliés* to her *pas de chats*, her *piques, batterie, change de pieds*. No wonder so many ballet steps are named after Mau — *pas de chat, entrechat, saute chat, quatre chat*. Her *ballon*, her elevations with no limbering at the *barre*, made a slob of me. I could tear my ligaments, wrench my back, split my toes, sweat and ache through years of practice and never leap velvet, take space like hoops of stretched silk.

Sapphira's sirloin snack was enough for one cat only, her tough-fibered voice warned me. Fat had to be trimmed, directions said. I cut deep into the red, sampling for possible fat, gnawed the bone to be sure no chips could choke her, snatched only one last morsel from her plate.

The King of Siam had trained his cats to be such good hunters that Sapphira retrieved. Her mouse was a green twist of pipe cleaner which I threw until my arm almost slipped its socket only to have her carry it back in her teeth and drop it at my red-stockinged feet, hers to bite and claw if a toe stirred like a mouse.

The way she had her will of space, leaping ten times her height, the spins, the turns, not a waste motion, a graceless attitude, perfection without aching a joint, *Prima Ballerina Assoluta* by right of birth.

When the Brandts turned the key in the lock, I was holding down Sapphira, studying the delicate articulation of her bones for her dancing secrets. "No mauling," said Mrs. Brandt, "although I can see how you might be carried away."

Freed, the cat caught a toe off guard. My yell brought Mr. Brandt to her defense. "The little one can't stand loud voices. We don't even allow ourselves to quarrel except in whispers. Her playful nips take you by surprise, I know. Best solution is to keep your shoes on after this."

"After this! There won't be any after this. I'm not suited to the job. I don't know cats — don't even think I like them."

"Oh, come," said Mr. Brandt, hairs standing out from his brows like cat's feelers, "don't be discouraged. She may take to you in time. Just follow her lead —"

"I don't like the way she stares — "

"You stare, too," said Mrs. Brandt. "We remarked how like Sapphira you are, with your blue-eyed stare. You even move alike."

My head lifted, ballerina proud, I could have done an *entrechat* on the spot.

"Life with Sapphira has many facets," said Mrs. Brandt. "Tomorrow she has an appointment with her couturier —"

"Is that what she calls her vet?"

"Feline *couturier*, costume designer. Sapphira has a fitting —"

"I don't know — I don't think —"

"She will pay a bonus for all such extras."

The shop in the East Fifties was marked by a sign Sapphira must have posed for. Bricks were painted shocking pink behind an iron gate left its usual black.

The boy in charge, his crew cut more fuzz than bristle, bucked his teeth to, "Baby — Sapphira jewel — how's my best girl?" and with no indication that I'd come in too, spread the latest in kittiemetics before his client — perfume blended with cat oils, brilliantine, sachets, glitter dust.

I had seen enough choreographers at work to know the throes when his eyes minnowed behind his lids, his hands groped air ... "For the promenade I see you in tangerine shading to palest yellow — perhaps just a fleck of gold, the merest fleck. For the soiree, chartreuse — chartreuse and silver."

As Sapphira sniffed and moused at a mink collar, he extricated it with, "No, baby, not for you — you're too ravishing in your own right. Mink is for mutts."

With hat boxes, dress boxes, accessory boxes, he enthroned Sapphira in the cab, leaving me to crawl in somehow.

Mrs. Brandt in the crackle of package opening never heard me give notice as I helped closet Sapphira's wardrobe. "Would you mind taking just a stitch on her little hankie pocket, dear? And if you'll brush an iron over her evening coat, tomorrow; she's modeling them Friday —"

"But I won't be here. I only said I'd —"

"Won't be here! Surely you're staying for what this is all about. They might want to use your hands holding Sapphira. If you play it right, it could mean modeling assignments for you."

The studio was blue-hot with lights that fried my already dry red hair during my act, not as a model, but as her lackey, ironing a last-minute ruffle, adjusting a collar, arranging pleats while she basked in tropic rays with a paw over her photogenic face, that no crawling on hands and knees among the snaking cords would cajole her to uncover.

"Now that I've seen you through this," I told the Brandts, "I must leave," but they sold me on the peace-with-pay of just sitting for a few nights, except for the Waldorf Astoria Fashion Show, which had possibilities. Anyone might be there — advertisers, newspaper men, show people. I could see Sapphira holding models at spitting distance, letting only me lead her down the runway to storming applause, flashing bulbs. I dressed her in her cocktail coat, sprinkled glitter dust in her hair, a bit in mine, but Sapphira queened it without me, making stooges of the human models.

I could learn from that cat. The way she rolled a marble about the floor, an excruciating lesson in toe work. Isadora Duncan searched for the secret of motion in her solar plexus, but I looked for it in Mau, Goddess of the sapphire rule. Mau, Mau, catch me up in your motion, and I'll be more than Markova, more than Fonteyn, I'll spin the globe to my toe point.

Motion — she was motion — motion as it was in the beginning, creation itself. One day in the capitals of the world, interviewers would be asking, "Who taught you?" and I'd say, "A cat was my teacher — yes, a cat."

In the exhilaration of her leaps I'd leave the towel rack to bend space to my will only to hobble over to the sofa, my spine in the grip of hot pliers as she went on with her boneless leaps. Again I'd agonize my muscles toward one *jeté* ribboned as hers.

Others could choreograph a cat the usual ear-scratching, face-washing way. I would choreograph Mau, source of all motion. Voodoo behind that evil mask, voodoo in the doll she clawed and bit and knocked the hell out of, voodoo in her whiskey howl, her evil wand of a tail. No dancer shall be as great as Mau.

Shut up alone with Sapphira night after night, while she sat as on an invisible throne cushioned by her own fur, I studied her as if she were the sole being left alive; microscoped from her spun-glass motions to her two tones, an intricate blend of lighter and darker hairs leading up to the seal dark and paling to silver under the throat. Why, her eyes were jewels beyond ours because they had no whites, they were all blue fire — ruby fire in the half light-eyes of Egypt. Who said cats have no noses to speak of? Her jet nose in profile, the cat of empire.

Her expensive odor got in my hair, my clothes, her two-tone hairs in my woolens. Every time I passed a faucet I flicked spite water at her to hell howls; juggernauted the vacuum cleaner toward her to devil spits; threw her around to prove she was a nothing in my hand, which I could more than wrap around her throat, and I fell to wondering why baby sitters do the things you read about — choke, smother, drown, hurl from windows. All hackneyed. In this oven of a place I smelled roast cat.

Back in my ice-box of a room, I still smelled cat roasting. Night shadows on the wall were Mau. In nightmares she was the Juggernaut, a great golden cat, its giant paw about to crush me, and I'd start, awake in a *barre* sweat, only chill.

On days off, Sapphira burned into my brain, put me through my job paces until I might as well be at her scratch and howl. Sapphira — I lived Sapphira, was Sapphira, except at the barre, where her mask mocked, the dance floor, where her elevations put me off balance.

An April evening warm enough to dally her through the park, I knew what I had to do. That didn't keep me from queening it with my fabulous cat brushed to cream and sable lustre, her tangerine collar and lead bringing tropical ripeness to a park in pale new green.

"Oh, beautiful"... words like a stirring of pigeons' wings ... "gorgeous" ... "bluest eyes" "May I pet her?" ... "just touch her fur?" ... "the grace" ...

All the same it had to be done. I kept on to the rock-ragged, gullied north end of the park, deserted after a series of muggings and murders. When she went on a sit-down, I carried her in careful cat-book style, her hind legs tucked in my hand. She purred. I took off her tangerine collar and lead, wrapped them in a newspaper lying on a bench, and with a stick, poked them deep into a trash can among orange peels and banana skins.

A man climbed the rocks above with two boxers off the leash. I turned a fast corner, the cat writhing and clawing; hurried through shadow thickets, every breeze starting them up at me from benches and side paths. A gang of boys shouted and pommeled, threw stones at a squirrel.

I cut off into the bushes, scratching my arms on the twigs, climbed a rock, the cat hell-howling; slid down the other side, crept into a dark hollow; let her loose, and ran — ran until my lungs were ready to burst.

Near the Sixties I slowed, my breath coming like some zoo animal, drank at the fountain by the closed carousel, saw her coarse tongue swollen with thirst, the grainy roof of her mouth turning into mine as a cat circle tightened about me, fire eyes, fangs, furious tails, never letting me quench my thirst, cool my face. I walked on to prove I could break the cat ring, but it moved with me live as Sapphira's boneless body. Cats' eyes fired the dark.

Scratchings in the underbrush — only a squirrel. Somewhere her eyes were lost fire in the night. The boys might stone her as they stoned the squirrel. Her tail would be mocked, mistreated in the streets. From behind a rock, I thought I saw a palm-sized head kittened to one side, but it was just a branch stirring to a breeze.

Lost off in her sable mittens. If she ever worked her way out of the park, she would join the underground, the alley cats who live their night life under parked cars. I'd watched a woman trying in vain to catch her lost cat in a net along that ghost alley.

Sapphira could howl hell and no one would set sirloin before her; her *port de bras* would be for garbage cans. One night in an alley, the cat book said, and her young would be alley cats, undoing generations of queens. No more Siamese.

The Brandts had to be faced before they threw a police dragnet around me. I let myself into the empty apartment, real only in its smell of cat, sat down to wait among the cat hairs of the sofa, steadied my hand to light a cigarette that couldn't bother her now even though her eyes gave me the blue burn from her oil portrait on the wall. I flung up the windows from the bottom, my glance dizzying down to the park below that crouched like a great cat ready to spring.

A confession note would be best, about how Sapphira slipped her collar, loose buckle perhaps, got lost. No, nothing in writing. Said words can bird-track every which way.

Sapphira's marble rolled to my pacing, her pipe-cleaner mice strewed the rug. I slipped off a shoe and tried to toe-flex the marble, cup it to precision under eyes of blue disdain.

"The window — the window —" Mrs. Brandt humped across the room on her sagging arches.

"Where's Sapphira?" Mr. Brandt waved his feeler brows. "She always hears the elevator."

"Well, something happened. She's — she's —"

Mrs. Brandt almost clutched the pearls off her throat. "The — the window?"

"No, it's just that she's lost somewhere in the park. She slipped her collar, the buckle must have come loose, and she was gone."

"Then why aren't you out there on your hands and knees trying to find her?" Mrs. Brandt caught at my arm. "Scratches."

"I hunted her through sharp underbrush. What are you suggesting — foul play?"

"Of course not," said Mr. Brandt, "you've no motive. We'd better notify the police, the park department. This requires an organized search."

Police department, fire department, park department, radio, television, newspapers, generous reward, nothing brought back the Brandts' solid-gold cat. No Sapphira in the known world, no fashion appointments, no press notices, no sitter — just a nothing of a lost cat. Now I am an entity once more — I am a dancer. I can take my place at the *barre*.

This without reckoning on Sapphira, not the vengeance of fang and claw, no hell spitting — beyond crime and punishment, serene on your self throne. Mocker at the *barre* as I sweat for what you have just by being. No ringing fame will ever be worth anything with your temple bell frosting a reminder that your motion is beyond me.

Eyes straight from the Book of the Dead. Lost in a park, you become the never lost, the living presence. You are Mau.

[*Prairie Schooner*, Summer 1955]

THAT INFERNAL LAST

THE BOSTON Shoe Show had taken over the Parker House, this week, making demands on shoe leather from kitchen to Grand Ballroom where models were dithering along the runway in somewhat frantic post-war styles.

Setting themselves somewhat apart from the shoe and leather men, the members of the National Association of Last Manufacturers felt the power of Genesis in their bones over the knowledge that the last comes first, and any play on words involving first and last was always good for a ritualistic laugh.

To an outsider, they were patient to explain that the last comes first because the shoe is made over this block of sugar maple carved to the outlines of the human foot, and if the shoe is to fit, the measurements of the last must not vary so much as a fraction of an inch.

Tonight the last manufacturers were giving a banquet in honor of Mr. Beaton, head of the Staunch Last Company, who was retiring after forty-seven years in the business. He was the president of their association, the man who had worked to unify their industry, who had set the tone of their advertising, articulated their policies. It was he who had helped to put many a foot-health law through the Massachusetts Legislature, who had fought for the natural last during an agony era of tooth-pick toes and high-buttoned torments.

Mr. Beaton was on his way to the speakers' table, his young man's walk at sixty-six a testimonial for the soundness of his lasts. The secret of youth is in the wood, he'd say. Not that his head and shoulders had a straight set to them. They urged forward in almost perpetual study of the treads around him, always a sorry look on his face at what he saw, a wistful wen working in the groove from nose to chin.

Some said he was the Savonarola of the worldly foot, exhorting the owners of deforming shoes to cast their unnatural vanities into the fire, and be saved.

At the moment, he had the responsible air of an official at a peace conference, carrying the world's foot troubles in his mental brief case, and prepared to tell the assembly that sound lasts have their part in keeping world peace. Children whose feet are tormented by ill-fitting shoes grow up full of suppressed hatred that any misguided leader can unleash. As can be seen every day in stores and buses, man's quickness to anger is often just an outcry against agonized feet.

"Your son, Travis, will be taking over, I suppose," said the President of the Lathrop Last Company.

"That's the general idea," said Mr. Beaton. "He's on his way home from the German occupation zone right now. Not that he has any special feeling for the last industry. Any business would do, so long as it brings in the money."

"Well, he's in the right business for that," said Mr. Lathrop. "There are two things people must have — bread and shoes."

Mr. Beaton bent over his plate of soup as if it were his first reward for a lifetime dedicated to the last. The warming soup, oak panels in the jeweled flash of chandeliers, even the carved plaster ceiling suggested the ease to come. Steam from the radiators hissed faintly against the first autumn frost until he felt an easy stretching along his limbs, a readiness to fall away from the tree and lie in the October sun. He had a right to feel like that now he'd won his fight for the natural last. College girls would be striding across the campus with broad, free tread; school children would go scuffing through the autumn leaves in shoes with plenty of toe room; young sprouts would go whistling along in lugger lasts and loafers.

The roast duck was just browned enough, and so tender he could cut it with a fork. He'd have time to go duck hunting now, if he wanted to, and perhaps take a few turns on the ice if he hadn't lost the knack.

Scooping up the orange gravy with a fork full of wild rice, he looked out from the spotlighted speakers table to the little satellite tables clustered beyond. His glance stopped off at a foot swinging in bronzed kid. What was such a last doing here, a needle-toed pump straight out of World War I, the very foot deformer he had spent his life defeating?

That twinkling steel-cut buckle probably hid the swollen flesh of an outraged foot, although her ankle was far from swollen as it led into the splendid calf that swung clear of the folds of her slashed dinner skirt. He worked his glance up to her face; not a sign of foot pangs yet even though she must be into her forties. Such a rich brunette pompadour made her mink stole look washed-out by comparison. Damn handsome woman, but that was aside from the point. Here it was a new era in lasts, and like the excesses of Rome in the flush of victory, this, this decadent last dared show itself.

Reddington was getting to his feet to introduce the first speaker.

Cigars were lighting up all around. Lathrop offered him one of his, but he couldn't sit back and enjoy it, not with that foot swinging right in front of him.

What was it he'd read in some trade paper? A lot of twaddle about the new era of elegance, lowered hemlines and rising heels, and here and there at openings, art exhibits, the ballet, a few discriminating feet could be seen in the slim, pointed pump that danced through the Irene Castle era. Is it the start of a new trend, the writer wanted to know, spreading from one or two custom shops to the entire world of fashion?

At the time he had dismissed the thing as a writer hard up for something to say. Yellow journalism, that's what it was, setting feet like this to swinging throughout the nation, as long as they could swing, that is, in such foot-deforming shoes.

"And the entire industry stands to benefit," Reddington was saying, "by Mr. Caudel's experiments in laminated wood." His voice sagged as something went wrong with the loud-speaker, then crashed against his eardrums as the apparatus went on again," ... wood that permits hitherto impossible accuracy, resistant as it is to the contractions and expansions of changing weather."

None of that laminated stuff for him, not unless considerably perfected. He'd take good, sound sugar maple. Why, he'd carved his first last out of sugar maple when his father had taken him out to Uncle Dave's last factory in Brockton. His uncle had put the rough block into his hands and showed him how like a sculptor's art it is to carve the master last from which thousands like it will be made, and he felt power in his hands as he smoothed and rounded the wood to the rhythm of interrelated curves, power to create a last for the feet of the world. It was something like a minister receiving a call-a light, a certainty.

He liked to go out on his own factory floor, sleeker than any ballroom from constant treading on the wax that dropped from lasts polished smooth as pearl-wood shavings spurting out from the machines like bursts of laughter; the last turning, turning and turning to perfection of contour while upstairs the artist among the workers was carving the master last by hand. Bins were always full, and he could reach down and perhaps turn up a last that would mold a ballerina's slipper, a last for a work shoe, a child's last, and as he held any one of them he held someone's fate in the palm of his hand. A last was a free walk through the countryside, the flash of a skipping rope, or a painful shoe kicked off in the dark of a theater.

Smell of wax and machine grease folded into the stout wood smell, he took it everywhere with him, in his clothing, his hands, his very pores. Wherever he was in the plant, even at his desk, he could feel the vibration of the machinery like a great ship in motion-his ship.

The steel-cut buckle glittered like a lot of malicious eyes, as her swinging foot mocked all he had tried to do until his life seemed little more than land falling away into the sea. Must she pick the night of his retirement to waggle that outrage at him? He'd like to snatch it off her foot and put it where it belonged, in his collection of historic shoes, labeling it 1919. Well, she was wearing it in 1947, and what's more, looking damn comfortable in it, but she'd see. Her great toe cramped in that bronzed kid was pointing toward the agony of an inflamed bursa.

His wife might have gone through life in foot misery if he hadn't caught her young and shod her right. Too bad she couldn't have lived to be here tonight in a dress last that would put this other woman to shame. Just sixteen in her high-buttoned white kids at the church strawberry festival. He discovered her slipping away past the Japanese lanterns at the edge of the lawn to the concealment of the big elm. By the time he reached her she was grappling with buttons that must have cut cruelly into her instep. As soon as she saw him she reached for a frail gold hairpin, and tried desperately to button up again.

Bending down as if to help her, he suddenly forgot all sense of decorum, startling her by working the buttons loose instead. He had to do a lot of explaining about the twenty-six bones in the human foot and the free play they required before he could convince her he was not being forward, and so get on with easing off her shoe and working over her foot to restore the circulation.

"I don't want to be unkind," he had said, "but you have quite a bit of breadth through the ball, and if you keep on wearing such unsuitable shoes — not that I can bear to mention anything so ugly in connection with you — but you'll end up with a — a bunion."

She winced a little at the word. Perhaps he should have said enlarged joint.

"Oh," she said, "I always thought they ran in families. My mother has one, and my grandmother, and the way my big toe has been feeling lately, I was beginning to think there was no way out for me, that is, until you came along."

"Tell you what," he'd said, as she looked up at him as if he were some new kind of god. "I'll design a special last for your foot, and have my father's factory make it up into a shoe for you."

Of course, as is likely to be true of any first design, that particular last had rather a clumsy look like the first cars and railroad engines. For their wedding, he had the style made up in soft white kid, but she put her own will first on that day, appearing in needle-toed deformers with white swan's feathers that might better be easing the soles of her feet than waving in front of the spectators. As for the heels, if they had been a fraction of an inch higher she would have pitched forward on her face.

Much of their wedding night was spent ministering to her feet, Epsom salts in hot water, hot as she could stand, a dash of cold, alcohol and massage. From then on, she planted her feet solidly, perhaps a trifle too solidly, in broad-balled oxfords.

Reddington was adjusting the mike before introducing the next speaker. "And now Mr. Phipps of the Ideal Last Company has a word to say on foreign markets in the post-war world. Mr. Phipps has just returned from ... "

Eddie Phipps had never given a single new idea to the industry, always scavenging the ideas of others. "Mr. Chairman," he was saying, "ladies and gentlemen, believe me it's a privilege ... "

Hard enough to educate your own children to correct lasts, let alone the world. Doris, a problem child all right — a weak-boned blonde wisp with creepy feet that slithered out longer when she stood on them, needing gentle but firm longitudinal support, but she insisted she had the narrow, elegant foot whose destiny was pointed toes. "But it's a weak foot, Doris. Your bones are weak. Besides, not even a narrow foot should wear toes that are too pointed."

If only she hadn't been so sneaky, but feet never keep a secret. He could tell whenever she had slipped out of the house in a forbidden last by the red marks on her pale skin.

First high heels caused something of a crisis with even his wife against him. "No high heels for a girl," she had kept dinning, "is like no first long trousers for a boy." Certainly he had tried to play along, even designing a special last for her first dance, and having the shoes made up in finest gold kid with built-in arch support and as trim lines as possible under the circumstances. "You can't dance if your feet hurt," he'd told her.

"I won't have anyone to dance with if I show up in these clodhoppers," she'd thrown back at him, but he'd seen to it that she appeared at that dance in the proper last.

He liked his family best when the children were little. Doris was a cute two-year-old clunking around in her papa's big shoes, and so fiercely fond of her own small slippers that she wanted to keep them on in her crib.

Saturday afternoon he'd take his little family shopping. Sometimes he wished there were at least eleven of them, all lined up getting new shoes. Children had the right wonder — the shy pride of older children in their new shoes, the little ones squealing with delight as they went skidding around in their slippery new soles.

Sunday was the best time, on their way to church-the boy's tread straight as an Indian's; Doris skipping on ahead; his wife's restful walk in the leafy shade; the sense of his own sure step. Sitting in their pew, he liked the rightness of the organ music, the ordered service, and his family in shoes that honored the human foot.

That woman was quite obviously turning to her companion and whispering, "Who was he?" Very well then, he'd ask, "Who was she?" He whispered to Lathrop who in turn asked the man next him. "Mrs. Edgecombe," relayed Lathrop, "some widow or divorcee the treasurer of the Foot Health Council is running around with."

What did that glance of hers mean anyway — from him up to the carved ceiling? Women were always misunderstanding his professional eye. He studied feet as a naturalist studies fauna and flora, and that nether stare of his, even the slight stoop, were identifying marks of his trade, he had told his wife, like the pallor of the baker.

In adolescence, though, even now sometimes, feet in impossible shoes would send his blood rushing along with steps that could only be hurrying to some secret rendezvous, and he'd imagine himself the waiting lover, bending down to remove her shoes, until he could almost smell the warm foot in the leather.

The buckle was a dizzying arc of light. Didn't that foot ever rest?

After the rich duck, the rocking motion made him rather sick to his stomach. Heedless women like that could overthrow all the good he had done. Well, he was out of it now. Let somebody else take up the fight. But who? Phipps, Lathrop, his son Travis? Could they talk shoe designers out of their own designs if they involved a poor distribution of wood? No, they'd let themselves be talked into making up a throwback like the last now cramping Mrs. Edgecombe's foot.

Reddington was about to introduce another speaker. Soon it would be his own turn. Maybe he'd better collect his thoughts — "It is with regret that I — with regret that I —" Damn that swinging foot. It seemed to be responding to inner music, perhaps an Irene Castle fox trot. Another foot used to swing like that. Where had he seen-on the Brockton train when business took him into Boston. He'd usually run across her on matinee days, and if there were ever an impossible shoe style perpetrated against the human foot, she'd be stepping along in it, dashing as a spanking team of horses waving their plumes.

She had a proud, shrugging way about her, but after a few seasons of such shoes she wouldn't be able to shrug off that growing foot condition. Her metatarsal heads were beginning to depress, and her big-toe joint was taking the unmistakable shape of a bunion.

Many times over, he wanted to speak, to warn her. Simple, if she'd been just anyone, but he was too attracted to be properly clinical. Women on the Boston Common, on a streetcar, a tired elevator girl, a mother with a youngster who wasn't treading just right, he could approach them, suggest help for feet not too far gone.

Sitting across from her one time, he had rehearsed desperately the words he should speak, but when he confronted her at the door of the train, her eyes fixed his in such round surprise, the brows seeming to add a segment of disdain, that he couldn't get the words out. Instead he took to designing lasts for a woman unaware of what she inspired, but he always hoped a way would be found to present the designs to her without giving offense.

Another time he saw that she was in the predicament she must always have dreaded. Her feet were puffed up like popovers, and when the train pulled into the station, the shoe she had slipped off wouldn't go back on. He could see the angry red joint of her great toe through her silk stocking. He urged and strained with her, watched her sit back flushed and breathless as the passengers began to hurry off the train. He began to search through his brief case as a pretext to stay behind. The conductor was going through the train calling "Last stop."

As she prepared for another painful tussle, he came forward to help, but she flung him a look that said, "I'll kill you if you dare to notice my humiliating predicament."

After that he gave up trying. Off and on for twenty years he watched those feet fail, watched her walk grow more and more painful. He could tell exactly when she had to seek professional advice — first appearing in orthopaedic contrivances that her lightweight shoes obviously had little room to receive, then in bluchers with contrivances, then alternated orthopaedics and dressy pumps, then just orthopaedics.

That's what this proud woman in front of him was walking into; only this time he ought to cry halt. But she was only one person. He should reach thousands like her, stop this dangerous trend before it started. Confound it, Reddington was introducing him already, preparing them all for his retirement speech.

"After forty-seven years in the business," Reddington was saying, "a man has earned time for his hobbies, especially if he is our friend Stuart Beaton, President of our Association, the man who has influenced the shoe styles of a nation, who has fought to put many a foot-health law through the Massachusetts Legislature, who has helped to impress upon the modern mind the importance of the last. Our industry can't afford to lose a fighter like Stuart Beaton, but what he has accomplished will always ... "

The woman was settling herself for a long siege of boredom, poising her bronzed slipper for a study of its slim contours.

"And now the boys, wanting you to know they're thinking of you every second of the time ... " Lord, what was Reddington holding out to him? Something gold all scratched up with names, a monstrous last with a clock set in an unholy bulge, as much of a sacrilege as a clock plunked down in the middle of a woman's abdomen, and he'd spent his life working against the unnatural, the

<141>

distorted. The golden calf must have looked like that to Moses when he came down from the mountain.

"Before you start carving any more names on that last, or pass it along to me as a retirement trophy, there's something I must say. Up to a few minutes ago I was going to touch on the usual — the long way the last industry has come since Civil War days when you couldn't tell a left shoe from a right because they were both made over the same last; the good feeling with which I could retire knowing that we'd won our fight for foot-conforming lasts — but something has come up to change my words. Now all I can conscientiously say is — I have no intention of retiring."

The stir was electric, all right. He looked towards the woman. At least she had left off contemplating her shoe, and was looking up at him.

"From now on I intend to fight. It's the same fight I put up just after the first World War, only like the second World War this second fight threatens to be more stubborn than the first."

She was leaning forward, adding her whisper to the general buzz.

"What is this fight that won't let a man of sixty-six retire? Most of us, here, remember the excruciating torture our wives and sweethearts went through when narrow lasts deformed their feet, but we've all taken it pretty much for granted that needle toes are as dated as whalebone and fainting spells. Well, those same lasts are trying to sneak back into favor.

"Certain fashionable women with nothing better to do than to overthrow the science of a lifetime are being seen in public in the very foot-distorting lasts we thought we had ousted. Custom-made as yet, soon they'll be seen everywhere, again deforming the feet of our sweethearts, our wives, our daughters."

Her foot had stopped swinging now, all right. "All women want what they see the exclusive few wearing; they'll besiege the stores, the buyers will seek out the shoe designers, and the shoe designers will come to us, the source, clamoring for lasts that are an offense against nature, and so it begins all over again, the feet of American women again enslaved, unless we fight. How can we write a lasting peace if we can't even protect the foot health of our nation? I mean to fight this thing, to rededicate my life to the creation of lasts that respect the rights of the human foot, and by an educational campaign to put the world on a sound footing."

The applause was beyond anything he'd ever stirred up before—storming, that's what it was — storming him into the fight. Hands in applause like a lot of turning lasts, the vibration of machinery, his ship in motion, and his blood was rushing through his brain a mile a minute rousing brain and muscle for the fight ahead. That woman wasn't applauding; she was scooching down in her chair, her feet tucked out of sight. Come now, he didn't mean to embarrass her publicly. He'd like to reassure her that in all the confusion probably no one noticed her shoes.

"Great speech, Stuart," Lathrop was saying. "Sure was dynamite," said Mr. Ardsley.

Others were piling up around him like a lot of lasts in a bin. Over their shoulders he could see the woman getting to her feet, alone now, her escort lost in the shuffle. As treasurer of the Foot Health Council, he was probably somewhere in the crowd waiting to congratulate him. A damn fine-looking woman, worth saving, and he wasn't going through another twenty-year shift without speaking up. By George, this was one woman he was going to save personally.

"Excuse me," he said as she started for the entrance, "someone I must catch." Sidestepping the group around him, he followed her out to the corridor, getting her attention just before she disappeared into the ladies' room.

"Haven't you made me conspicuous enough?" she said. "I catch the drift. My shoes are real shockers. They threaten to undermine American womanhood, and this very minute they're doing dastardly things to my feet, not that I feel the least physical discomfort."

"That's just it," he said. "Often you feel no pain at first, but if I were to exert a little pressure on your metatarsal heads, chances are you'd feel certain twinges."

She stood uneasily, shifting her weight to the other foot. "There, you see," he said, "you're already favoring one foot. Can you deny you feel leg pains, and perhaps smarting on the soles of your feet? I don't think you realize what a delicate mechanism you're trifling with when you go against the natural lines of the human foot." He was taking her arm, and leading her down the corridor. "There are just twenty-six bones in the human foot all set to do a magnificent

<143>

job if you'll let them. The arches alone are an engineering marvel, but once they break down —"

"Maybe I shouldn't give in to you so easily," she said, clasping both gloved hands around his arm, "but I must confess I've been getting sharp twinges lately, really excruciating sometimes, just under my instep."

"Your metatarsal heads. If several are depressed, soon the entire structure will collapse."

"What can you suggest?"

"The proper last without delay."

"No, no, I mean —"

"I know — some doubtful contraption that you can crowd into these same deforming shoes."

"Sounds silly the way you put it, but still —"

"Tell you what I'll do. I'll work out a last specially for your foot, one that will keep that look of slim elegance" — he glanced from her sable shining hair to the bronzed kid — "and still let your foot follow its natural lines."

"Rather broad lines, I'm afraid."

"Just the same, I'm sure something can be worked out."

"The way to intrigue any woman," she said, "is to promise something designed especially for her. My coiffure, my cosmetics, my— Well, we won't go into the basics, but everything I have on is supposed to be designed especially for me, and now my lasts, and by the most important man in the industry. But say, where are we going?" she said as they started down the steps to the lobby. "After all, I did come with someone."

"But you don't want to go back into all that confusion. Besides, if I know your escort, he'll be in there talking half the night."

They went out the School Street entrance. "I'd say let's walk a bit," he said, "if those poor slippers could take it." Instead he helped her into a cab, and as she eased off her shoe at the heel, he took a pencil out of his pocket, and on the back of an old envelope started sketching the new last.

[*Prairie Schooner*, Fall 1947]

HERE AM I

THE BAY WINDOW of her father's study opened like tables of stone to the mountain. Isaiah would be her text, this Sunday, not a cautious line or two, but an entire chapter, "Who hath measured the waters in the hollow of his hand . . . and weighed the mountains in scales, and the hills in a balance?"

Late-afternoon light was vining the snow, holding fast to the stone fountain, tightening around branches, footing the icy rail by the terrace where her spread arms used to make angel wings in the drift.

Youngsters banging down their sleds coasted her away with them, wind whizzing, snow stinging, toiling up for the swift down until the light of her father's study would reach her in surely as her name across the snow, *Genevra-Gen-ev-ra*, call to study hour, the Bible with him, call while the hill was swift. Whiz down one more time, street lights clicking on, one more time, runners cutting into their hour, his loneliest with Mama gone unless she came in to him.

The Bible in her father's voice had been thunder on the mountain, the Red Sea parting, the Persians storming the gates, prophets crying, "The grass withereth, the flower fadeth, but the word of our God shall stand forever."

Through every Bible passage, with the shouts of the coasting hill swifting her away to flight of ice, she had been as Jeremiah saying, "Behold I cannot speak; for I am a child" ... "Say not I am a child; for thou shalt go to all that I send thee .... "

Aunt Fay's shovel was chinking after coal for a furnace more ravenous than warming. Street lights would soon be clicking on, but she wouldn't spill out the light of her lamp like a bottle of yellow water-color across the snow staining the coasting hill deep into some youngster's memory. Light would silk through the drawn shades of her bedroom as she dressed for Gordon's coming.

Aunt Fay was still flirting ribbons at the thought that Gordon in his supercharged Chevy would scale the glass mountain and bear her off at thirty-three to his parsonage in the foothills, when a week from Sunday she was to be ordained and installed as pastor of her father's church.

The mountains in their darkening were the shoulders of her father in some vast sky pulpit. Spread-winged in his black robe he had made this little Adirondack pulpit great, ministering to his own people yet reaching those from the world below who came for fashionable summers. National figures had sat in his pews; his folders bulged with their letters; the Sermon on the Mount above his desk was painted by a distinguished artist.

Leslie had brought her to the world of summer people, walked her up the hill, the summer they were seventeen, to a glass house over the lake, words light as the flick of a fan, dancing that showed up her thick legs made to push through drifts in parish calls with her father. The Huntley bones had been bestowed on her in all their heaviness, the Huntley face, character in her father, pug-ugly in her unless she made an animated cartoon of it.

Alone with Leslie, she was no more awkward and uncertain than he, the summer woods, the lake, raining down fire not of the Gospel, an alarming kind of fire that brought them so close they must marry, run off together, only she didn't get very far down the road.

Soundless as his call on the coasting hill, soundless through the— Light sprang up in her face like a branch. "What are you doing here in the dark, child?" — Aunt Fay's cream-pudding voice — "Better be getting dressed. Gordon will be here sooner than you think."

On his way to her, up a mountain of ice. In a more romantic clime he'd be the kind to strum a guitar, throw a rose; yet everything in him that delighted her as a lover made her doubt his force as a minister. He would go with his congregation instead of leading them; charm them into church; coax them into heaven. Mustn't let him get her to such a fever point that she'd forget she was dedicated ... "Before thou earnest out of the womb, I sanctified thee, and I ordained thee." Not wife of one, mother of a few, but servant of all. His whispered words had been getting in the way of her work, his image coming between her and her congregation; she was dreaming instead of visioning.

She ran up the stairs with a pause at the landing, not to look out the red pane to the signs and portents of a ruby world, the way she used to when it was Leslie, but only to catch her breath. The telephone on the window seat had always been something of a tower of Babel when the aunts were three, and they stood above stairs while she was at the phone, urging her out and away, and Father stood below stairs reminding her that she had studying to do, their voices making hers sound frantic, words on the other end lost. Maybe without the widowed aunts, she could have been a bright-plumaged bird in her wing-spread to eternity instead of crouching in dread of a dark forest of days alone.

Her ordered room that had begun to settle like a shawl about her shoulders, could still be flung off in dressing for a date. She scattered powder in fragrant cloud, rushed through underthings laid away as too filmy for mountain cold, armed aside ungainly woolens, the aunts had knitted too large even for her.

In the back of the drawer, her fingers caught on the soft-harsh stuff of her mother's glitter scarf, once part of dream play in the secret dark, touching bare shoulders as she sat up against the headboard that was a gold ballroom chair, a throne.

She let down beige braids wound high for the pulpit, brushed them about her shoulders like Titian's Magdalene. Leslie had seen the fullness of her hair; Gordon must see it. She would coil it low in her neck; fasten it so lightly that it would shake down about her shoulders.

Her night lipstick was so seldom used, she couldn't find it anywhere in the drawer. The day lipstick was nothing but a tinted pomade against chapping. So few rites she knew, were beauty rites. She had only just caught onto tweezing the hairs that made her brows clownish; trusted the wind for color that flared and died. The night lipstick rolled out from under a pile of handkerchiefs. She flamed it on the characterful Huntley mouth, pressing the upper lip against the lower as she had seen a soft-mouthed demonstrator do.

The taffeta bronzed through the milky plastic of the garment bag, a dress to whisper around delicate bones like her mother's. Large bones got along better with plaids and woolens.

Gold metal beads gave her goose flesh until her throat began to warm them. Her gold mesh belt was ice, too. Accessories left over from seminary days. Not one of the divinity students could stand up to her father. As guest lecturer, he would stand before them, his eyes gray cloud gatherers, the eyes of mountaineers, seeing beyond, seeing heaven's light, seeing face to face. Those who said she had his eyes could only mean gray like his, set wide like his, for they were not so much his as looking after him.

Suave lover Gordon would come to the parsonage to learn from her father, yet preach toward the big-city pulpit. "Towns weren't something you graduated from," her father would say when called to a bigger parish. "Talent will always be knocking at those pulpit doors. It's here they need you." No worship service was ever rote on her father's lips. Her words must be as his, *live* as the day they were said by the shores of Galilee. If she married Gordon she must silence her father's voice to his, take her place in his Sunday-school room as a kind of doll lampshade over the light.

His car — its chains were clashing against the ice of the steep drive. In the sound of it, she was fleeing from more than going towards, fleeing like Jonah from the voice of God, fleeing from hours alone with the Book — years alone — fleeing from a light too strong to bear, a mountain pointing to eternal life before she had lived the days of her youth.

Gordon's step was somewhat cautious along the ash-strewn ice; her father would have charged up in his ancient arctics. In the hall mirror she quick-silvered a glance at herself as he removed his stadium boots with cavalier grace — mirror that slimmed and softened until in the whisper folds of taffeta she half expected emergence of her mother's finely articulated bones instead of an overgrown chick all but breaking out of the bronzy shell.

Pulpit art in every gesture, Gordon held out a gift, wrapped white and satin, much like a wedding cake to dream on. "A pocket warmer," he said, as she slipped the heated metal from its black felt case. "Carry it around in your purse to toast your fingers. It works by catalytic action."

A chill spread through her from her aunts' length of days when they trudged up to bed with warm soapstones; saved bits of string, gift wraps, buttons and buttons, clothes which saved long enough would come around to being in style again.

The warmer, held tight, pulsed in her hand. Gifts from her father, never for charm, either, years of gifts — dictionaries, concordances, interpretive Bibles. Their games, Bible cards; sermons, her dramatics, a chair for a pulpit.

Going in to dinner, Gordon slipped his arm about her waist, calculating her heft, then minimizing it like the gold mesh belt she had clasped about her thick diaphragm in dreams of a small waist.

In her father's chair at table, he looked almost bird-boned. Father had always made him appear shorter, almost wizened from smile lines that had set like sand flats to rather pleasing ripples. The

Huntleys, built for earth, looking toward heaven. Hers a child-bearing strength given over to parish calls, glorying in her strength, wind driving her along, glorying in it for his ministry; turning her hand to people's chores, shelling peas, washing dishes, taking a turn at the tractor . . . "Ye shall serve God upon this mountain" ....

Aunt Fay, ready for a chariot of fire to whirl the lovers away to the foothills before the ordination, started them for the drafty living room, muddy gold and purple, stiff-backed and horse-haired. Aunt Fay had coquetted around with cushions and hassocks, Spanish shawl for the square piano, incense for the fireplace. About all of her mother left in here was the cabinet with her collection of perfume bottles, and the china tea set she had painted gold and violet. A room in which you had to run interference against piles of magazines and newspapers her father had never got around to reading, stacks of books the shelves wouldn't take.

They sat before the fire on Aunt Elizabeth's hand-hooked rug, piney tar and incense folded into the left-over fumes of roast veal.

"I was going over Father's sermons, and I found a text you could adapt to —"

"Look, Genevra, I didn't struggle up your confounded mountain of ice to sit by the fire and talk about what a great minister your father was." His rough-edged grace swinging her into his arms, drifted her along with, "Come away with me."

Her aunt was trying to soft step along the hall to the dark reaches upstairs, but her step was Huntley heavy, time heavy, in its long climb, her own step climbing the years if she didn't come away with him. She'd be winding her father's clocks, the loose-strung clock in the kitchen, the grandfather's clock whose rising moon used to glimpse the world beyond, querulous china clock in the upper hall-growing old winding them, iron-grey old. In the strength she wanted to be held, strength beyond all thinking, she clasped him. His lips thrust hard — fingers along her throat deepened to her breast — "Come away with me. They'll never need you as I need you, nor cherish you as I do."

Thoughts rushed in about the withdrawal of his lips. "But the installation is fixed, church calendars printed, ministers invited, and they've all accepted save you — "

"No, you'll never see me at your ordination. I won't be there at the Laying on of Hands —"

Gordon was throwing his voice around with all the trumpeting of a one-time elocution teacher, a voice that thrilled her even though she knew it was trained in its effects.

"You wouldn't run out on your church once the installation date was set."

"The pulpit won't be empty. Fred Kearns is willing to act as a supply until they can call someone, and quite the reverse of suffering hurt feelings, they'll light up at a romance."

"These people need me more than you think."

"It's the pulpit you can't give up — being the great *I am*. The Sunday-school room isn't enough; working as my helper won't do—"

"Sunday school with sash and hair bows —"

"If it's the pulpit you want, I'll let you take mine sometimes, if you'll conform your sermons a bit to our pattern in a — well, a more sophisticated church."

"The pulpit *sometimes*. It's not for *sometimes* when you've been called. God has called me, and I believe his call is here, in my father's pulpit. This is where I must be."

"Back and forth — same old arguments back and forth. It's too late for that, Gen. Run upstairs, pack your suitcase, and we'll drive to my sister's house tonight. If I let you deliberate, you'll never break away. All we have to do is send a wire to Fred to take the pulpit Sunday. We can be married within three days."

Her father's pulpit — hers in trust — her *call*. Her steps knew every uneven board of this old church. Here they kept him alive, within these pews, along this aisle, before these altar steps.

"You've been lonely here, Gen. There's no place lonelier through the long winter. Those who can, get away."

"That's why I must be here."

Silence was as doors closing — storm door, hall door, inner door to the winter dark, to sounds of an old house settling. Fierceness of her grasp startled him out of his restrained lovemaking to a hold that loosened hers until she felt molten, fashioned anew in his arms.

The fingers of his hand stopped short of knowing her, left her shaking before the fire. In the long years aging she would huddle just here, warming herself at this recall. A body like hers would gnarl into the nineties alone. The old smell would be in her

<150>

bedroom, the old smell of her aunts among their salves and lotions, body acids through flannel gowns.

"Gen, I'm sorry if I — well, if I hurt you." He was lighting his cigar, velveting it into pine tar and failing incense, a thin-lipped city-pulpit seeker with clipped cigars and clipped speech. It would be a swift downflight with him from the light and the life, the work and the word.

His chariot of fire was burning out. He lifted himself up from the rug to get an early start down the icy hill. Standing away from the hall mirror that was cold-lighted like a ticket window after hours, she watched him bundle himself away from her in muffler and great coat. She threw a plaid stole about her to go to the storm door with him. Ice clouds refracted the light of the moon to ghostly rainbow traceries. Their breaths trembled white in good-byes. Smell of pine needled the air. Bushes were bursting with snow blossoms. She could bury her face in them, sink into burning, stinging drifts, ice gone to fire, caught up by them, borne away. She switched on the porch light for his going, and in his backward look at the foot of the steps, she saw how she must appear to him, like her aunt waving her off to the seminary, the one left in the frail-lighted doorway.

His tire chains cut into the rutted ice as she shivered deeper into her stole waiting for his final wave at the turn of the hill. Chains fainter as from a hollow in the mountain, she switched off the porch light, forced the storm door shut, locked and bolted the hall door, and going through to wind the kitchen clock, gave the swinging door of the dining room the thrust she used to as a child in a dark-panicked moment to bring the one light through to the turning on of another.

Aunt Fay came down to the landing in her dim-flowered robe— brows asking.

"No, Aunt Fay, nothing came of it. How could anything come of it, with the installation date fixed?"

Alone in her room, she fingered the red mark at the fullness of her throat where he had drawn blood to the surface so gently that she hadn't realized his kiss was bruising. She unclasped her gold beads, and laid them away in the jewel box. Tomorrow she would put the disordered bureau to rights.

In the dark she drew in against the old house settling and shrinking about its core. Weight of snow fell from the roof like the lightest dusting of timpani, words diamonding through its drifts ... "Father of lights with whom is no variableness nor shadow of turning" ... Father of lights ... Father of lights ....

Over breakfast, next morning, Aunt Fay tossed confetti words about ... "Gordon's not one to give up, Gen. He's just dramatic enough to snatch you away at the last moment. Mark my words."

Mark her words — mark her words out of here across the snow-drifting path to the church. Snow was sun in unbearable radiance like the white light that struck Paul blind on the road to Damascus.

Last Sunday's hymns were still numbered on the board of the empty church. Light through the honey-pale windows spread along the milk-white walls and across the pews to touch the wine-red carpet shabby — faithful like her father's shoes that were sealed in the timbers of her faith. Mounting to his pulpit, she looked out across emptiness; beat her hand against the oak; beat, bruised. Not set on high in a lonely pulpit; not set on high. Gordon would still come for her; one phone call, and he'd come, bring her away with him, away from serving God upon this mountain. Her steps took her down from the pulpit, but only to the altar where she knelt to His will. ...

The days that were left to her, she closed up with busyness as tightly as she could. The night before the ordination after she had gone up to her room with a glass of warm milk to help her sleep, Aunt Fay called her to the phone, Gordon's voice flickering through the ice-laden wires ... "Gen, why not be ordained tomorrow, but not installed? Of course you want to be ordained after all your work and study, but you don't have to be installed as minister of the church."

"But I've been called — called not only to the ministry, but to this church. I can't close my ears to —"

The click of his receiver cut her off . . . "Gordon," she sent across the dead wire ... "Gordon" ....

Morning was heavy with snow about to fall. In sighing attendance, Aunt Fay helped her to dress for the ceremony with the care of a bride, laid out her best slip with its depth of lace, her black pulpit gown, brushed her hair smooth for the Laying on of Hands. They crossed the newly cleared path to the white church festooned with icicles, the arbor hung with snow roses, a sun you could look full on, honey-pale in a milk sky. Stevie was out with his beginner's sled, trying it down the Eckharts' terrace.

The organ sent out its stained-glass colors to the snow as Mrs. Rierson practiced the Handel she would be playing just after the prayer of ordination, and in its stilling, Dean Stafford would say for her father, "We hereby declare you to be duly ordained and set apart," and it would be her father's voice saying, "Ye shall serve God upon this mountain."

The service was as the ringing of bells, carrying her through to the words, "Are you now ready to take upon you this holy ministry and faithfully serve in it?" ... and her own voice rising to a bell tone ... "I believe, and am ready, God being my helper."

"Will you tend the flock of God committed to your care, taking the oversight thereof not by constraint but willingly?" ... words falling about her like snow on the mountain . . . "I shall so engage, God being my helper."

In the Laying on of Hands, she knew her father's hand to be upon her head; heard his voice speaking through Dean Stafford, "We hereby declare you to be duly ordained and set apart" ....

Through her father she would ascend to the pulpit, and the rain of fire would come down from beyond the mountain as the words she would speak. If ever she were called like her father to pulpits in the cities below, she would stay here in the mountains. They must come to hear her where her father's hand stretched forth. She had put him on with the pulpit gown, put on the father ... God, the Father ....

[Prairie Schooner, Fall 1952]

CUP OF GOLD

MRS. HOLBROOK opened her cabana so early, the sun was just hazing through to the sea. Troubled, troubled, she had to walk — walk furiously up the shore.

"Want to walk with me?" she called to Mrs. Demarest.

"I know your walks, Wilma. My short legs can't keep up."

"Well, then, come sit with me. I'll make some coffee."

Mushroomed under straw, Mrs. Demarest looked up at Wilma's length of line. "You're the youngest grandmother anywhere around. That race-horse figure topped off with brown eyes that glitter like the sea — Mrs. Conant says you're the most stunning —"

"Now stop trying to marry me off. If you lost a pearl, would you pick up a pebble?"

"A great man, the Judge, but that's no reason to burn on the pyre. You have your son."

"I'm not sure of the girl he let himself become engaged to —"

"Have I seen her out here?"

"Why, I haven't even met her."

"A showgirl or some model? Such affairs are always going pouf. I remember when my Jack —"

"Worse."

"A different religious faith?"

"That, too, I suppose." Wilma poured Mrs. Demarest a cup of coffee. "You'll need a strong cup when I tell you he's involved with a Puerto Rican."

They observed silence on the dune as the sea moved in with its breaking waves.

"Puerto Ricans aren't the worst mixture, Wilma. Spanish and Indian, mostly, and a fine breed of Indian, I read, a peaceful tribe who fled to Puerto Rico from the cannibals. The Spanish blood could be even better than ours. I read that royal families in search of adventure settled Puerto Rico. She could be royalty."

"Drool. My husband and I cruised the Caribbean. Most of these natives aren't down out of the trees yet. She wants to marry her way into the United States. That's what she wants."

"But P.R.'s are American citizens. She can come anyhow."

"By way of the slums. I do enough social work to know what East Harlem is like — heroin users in every hallway, pimps, child prostitutes. Generations have gone into forming sons like ours, and just as he is about to finish law school, she has to cha cha into his life —"

"How did they happen to meet?"

"Her family sent her to some unknown college round about. Lynn met her at one of those week-end affairs. You lavish a lifetime on a son, and in a weekend it's all undone."

"Perhaps he loves —"

"Love — love — love — lust, more like."

"I'd say it was a rebound from Alexis. He wasn't quite up to her."

"What do you mean, not quite up to her?"

"She needs — well —"

"I know — someone more dynamic, like my husband. Lynn will never be a public figure, he's more behind the scenes. The boy has his father's height, but not his presence. Nothing I can say can keep him from standing as if he were apologetic over his six-three."

"Well, your husband probably developed his court presence over the years."

"No, he had the same command at twenty-two. Lynn has my husband's reflectiveness, though. He may well accumulate a body of writings the way his father did, a philosophy of jurisprudence.. He may never be the jurist his father was, but he dearly loves the law. He plans to be a tax law authority. What's the use of anything now that he has thrown himself away on that Puerto Rican?"

"Don't worry — these sudden affairs have a way of breaking like a Christmas tree ornament."

"That's what I'm living on."

"There is a way," Mrs. Demarest slyed up, peering over her coffee cup, "to put her in a different light. I've dealt with something like this."

"How?"

"Well, when my daughter had a case on her ski instructor, I invited him to stay with us here at Westhampton Beach, to show him up away from the ski slopes — his language, his table manners, his —"

"And how am I supposed to show her up when she is in San Juan? He's visiting her family before his summer school starts at Columbia. It sends cold chills up my spine even in this heat, fearing a *fait accompli.* What if he marries her down there? Excuse me, I've got to walk — walk fast and furious."

She ran down the beach stairs, crossed sands warming to the sun, walked the cool of the surfed shore rushing it to footprints that were being sneaked away behind her back, footprints, footprints, and footprints, in disappearing aspic.

TROUBLE slowing her pace to Lynn's long-legged stroll. His first weekend with her here at the beach club after the San Juan jaunt. So in love with the morning he shaded his eyes to the sun-soaring of a gull, stooped to a moon shell, a pebble.

"Lynn, how would you like to start your law career in the grand old firm of Allison and Hughes, in their tax department?"

"Who says I'll pass the bar exams?"

"I know — you're letting the legend of your father get in the your way. I had to work just as hard with him as I do with you, hearing his exam material over and over instead of dancing off to shows and parties. Do you know what you father said just before he — he died? He wasn't much for words, just a judicious few, but he said, "I couldn't have done it without you, Wilma. I've seen more young lawyers held back by wives even slightly unsuitable than —"

"Not that old play-back, Mother."

"You know how it was — the entertaining and the civic activities expected of me as Justice Holbrook's wife when I would rather be out here walking the tideline, taking the waves. It's a career being a wife to a distinguished man."

"Which I am not and never will be."

She reached up to his salt-sea mane, looked into eyes the grey of his father's blue. His father's hair almost unjudge-like in its mane curl, Lynn's thinning a bit at the crown for one so young.

"All I ask is that you know her better. Your father and I were engaged for three glorious years when we found we not only loved, we liked each other. Our marriage was good because we prepared for it."

"Some love is fragile — it will wing away if you wait too long."

"Admission right there that you're only flying on butterfly wings, if you can't wait until you are graduated in May."

"Sure, put the butterfly on a pin."

"Why, it's less than a year. If a hundred thousand were deposited to your account for waiting a few months —"

"What is this? *Camille*[9] — Holbrook version?"

"Ridiculous. If there's anything worth having between you, waiting will only deepen it. And you don't have to wait to be willed your uncle's rare editions. He says you should be concentrating on your bar exams, and it's worth parting with his rare editions to see that you do."

"That's below the belt, Mother. I grew up wanting those books — they're people, plump leather people. You mean he'd turn them over to me just for waiting until I'm graduated?"

"That's right."

He leaped satyr into the surf.

MOST CABANAS were winter-closed after Labor Day. Wilma looked down the empty row. Trash cans were crammed with crushed straws, torn bathing-caps, wilted swim suits. The dune had its leavings — broken kites, dented sand pails, a little red fire engine. Up the beach as, down the beach as far — no none — yet the sun had a bite, and the surf was summer-warm. The people in the locked section weren't so quick to jerk down summer like a kite. Mrs. Spencer was coming up the ramp in her flowered bathing suit.

"How about walking up the shore with me a ways?"

"Let's make it a swim, Wilma. I can almost keep up with you with my swimstroke."

Wading out, Mrs. Spencer asked Wilma, "Did my idea work?"

"Which idea?" *Plan B: The 'other woman' disaster, of course.* "Oh, you mean exposing him to somebody else? Yes, in a way, he discovered her himself, at summer school, a fellow law student, but I did all the furthering I could. It was good to hear law-talk in the house again. They had quite a few dates together, mostly in law courts. Just as Lynn seemed to losing his heart to her, she told him she was in love with a married man."

"Poor Lynn. He has bad luck with his girls, except for that — that —"

---

[9] *Camille.* Refers to the interfering parent who prevents Armand's marriage to Camille in Dumas' drama, *The Lady of the Camelias*, basis for the opera *La Traviata* and the Greta Garbo film *Camille*.

"*Please!*" She swam out to the barrels, and beyond. Not thinking, not thinking about *that*.

When she let the waves surf her to shore, Mrs. Spencer was still there, sunning herself on the sand. "Sure you don't want to walk up the beach?"

"Not me — the sun has me in a net." She paused, eyes drilling her. "You mean none of your ideas worked with Lynn?"

"None — I'm sick over it — literally — I was awake half the night with stomach pains. I suppose I'm too knotted up to digest my food. They've even set a date — the twenty-seventh."

"Of?"

"Of *now*. This month — September."

"In San Juan?"

Wilma winced. "No, her family is arranging a wedding here at the Waldorf Astoria."

"Then they must have means. She's not marrying for money."

"The girl is still bettering herself. My late husband's quite considerable estate — our position —"

"She may not be too impossible. They have given her a college education here in America, and you told me the father is an architect."

"But they give themselves big titles down there. They throw 'Engineer' around the way some countries do 'duke' and 'count.' If he so much as slaps mortar on a brick, he's an architect or Minister of Housing."

"Even if you came to accept the girl, supposing she's not too dark, the child could be fine, a throw-back —"

"I know — I know — it's tearing out my insides."

"I suppose you'll have to attend the wedding, since it's being brought to you."

"Lynn and my maid Hilda, how they conspire. Assuming I'm going, arranging my things behind my back. I'm sick inside.

"But do you know know what my daughter did? She phoned me all the way from Seattle to say she is making arrangements to come — *after the wedding*. When they're off on their honeymoon, that's when she's coming, she said, to be with me when I'm most alone."

"If it's nothing but animal attraction between them – on again, off again once already, you see — then this affair may still blow up before the twenty-seventh."

"It's my fierce hope." She turned and started down the shore on her solitary walk — fast — fast and far.

WILMA SAT LOOKING out over the late September sea, not up to her walk today, certainly not up to a swim in those crashing waves. Such pains in her stomach, like fists punching, she feared ulcers. More like, a pot of poisons brewed against this — this dark-skin. The cabana mirror should be throwing back her face algae-green instead of oak-leaf tan.

One. One week before the wedding — one week for something to happen. Canaria already here with friends. The P.R.'s would soon be parakeeting about their Waldorf suite, too dizzy with wedding plans to embarrass her out here, Hilda buzzing into the phone just out of earshot in pretend compliance.

"Mother? Mother?" Lynn's voice caverned across the empty pool below.

"Up here, Lynn."

"Be prepared for a great surprise. Canaria is with me."

A stomach pain doubled her over the way she had imagined the swimmer's cramp. If she had been in water, she would surely have drowned. "Lynn — wait —" She squeezed out through her pain. "I'm not — feeling — too well. Better wait till —"

Up the ramp before she could finish her sentence, the girl behind him like a camp follower – a wonder she wasn't carrying a pack.

"Mother, if you knew how I worry when you insist on swimming in that autumn ocean without life guards. What if you had a cramp like this, out there?"

The pain eased enough to let her straighten to her height above the girl.

"Mother — Canaria. Isn't that a lovely flower name? It means cup of gold."

"Oh?"

"Well, I'll leave you two while I have the car checked. I don't like the sound of the motor."

Canaria there, in the going-away of Lynn, was a kind of drowning, a dizziness back to the tides of Grand Central station just before her own wedding, not feeling up to being his wife, to meeting his distinguished family even though her own people were first in their Indiana town.

"Sit down, won't you? Would you like a cup of coffee?" Her voice shaking out like a tight-rolled umbrella.

"That would be delightful."

The Nortons moled up the ramp from their locker rooms to see what was going on above stairs. What was she gaping at? The girl's skin was lighter than their thick coffee tans. Canaria — cup of gold.

"Let's have some music." She motioned to a chair, sheltering Canaria away from sideshow stairs, just as the radio would blur them from overhearing. She paused at the dial uncertainly. "There's a Spanish station, if I can find it."

"Is there a — a 'UXR'?"

"Oh, you mean WQXR. Why, that's my one and only station."

Of course, the poor thing couldn't say "double-u" — a letter not in her Spanish alphabet. Good English, though, with the charm of an accent.

That's what got him, every word fresh as pique, and a face that moved in on you. It seemed to come out of her own mirror — not feature for feature, no patrician bones. She was Indian broad of cheek, her lip rolling sweetly forward, eyes wideset to a lighter brown than her own. Style, too, in her Carib way, a rather fixy silk suit, hand-embroidered blouse, a fussy flower hat atop hair with a marcel wave like her own in the twenties.

Brahms in full tide over WQXR almost too swelling much, the sea and the music of Brahms. She, herself, the one in tears like a Carib all emotion while Canaria sat contained, yet her broad face had its first beauty in the Brahms. They listened with a oneness she had wanted from her own daughter.

Now it was the nosy Gannons finding excuses to run up and down the ramp. She would never let them intrude on this moment. Let them squint from their distance at a girl with all the graces she had tried to give her own blunt daughter, the repose of manner she had wanted for herself, the Professor's gangle-boned child.

So at one after the Brahms, letting the waves merge the themes that she had to shake herself out of the timeless to the present question. "Do you play any musical instruments?"

"The piano — a little. I'm working on a Brahms Ballade."

"Then you play more than a little —"

"He is so — so *un*piano, my hands cannot stretch to the chords. Chopin is more for my fingers. Do you play? You have beautiful hands for Brahms."

"Well, thank you. Lynn is always remarking on my hands. I rather envy those who are creative, but somebody has to be audience."

"Listening, it seems to me, is most creative — brining your own imagination to what you hear."

"Do you think that, really? I never thought of myself as in any way creative before. You must play for me sometime. We have a grand, almost concert-size, autographed by Gieseking."

"Gieseking! — His Debussy — I have all his Debussy records."

"A musical talk like this is so — so satisfying. Canaria, how would you like to give a talk at my Civic Club on Puerto Rico — its music and anything else of interest."

"I'm afraid I would disappoint you as a speaker. Perhaps Lynn could do it from my notes. There is so much to know about our island. You're Episcopal, too, Lynn tells me. Saint Thomas's was the first Episcopal Church to be established in the Americas."

"Why, that's fascinating. You needn't think of it as a lecture, just talk to us in your own words. Let's walk up the shore a ways."

"This I would love. The Atlantic up here has waves like a great pipe organ. I must learn to swim your ocean. Lynn tells me you are a strong swimmer with such long-armed grace."

"He said that? He never told me any such thing. I'll teach you how to take these waves." She started whipping up the shore, Canaria panting along like a puppy you can't lose. Then she slowed and stopped. Why walk fast anymore, with the threat panting alongside?

After a litltle while they paused, and Canaria knelt to a backwash of crystal jellies, fingered their beaded rays to the sands of her island. You could love a man, be excited over the new surroundings, yet still be alone. In that moment, the young woman was alone with her own sky and sea. So she knew the power of solitude.

Obviously, Canaria had no need of their wealth, their position. Lynn was probably the closest Canaria had ever come to a man, like the man she had married. Her arm went around Canaria.

Walking back, in and out of surf reach, she scaled her legs to Canaria's attempts at longer steps, quickened to Lynn coming down the shore, his mane in a sea-tangle.

Nothing Lynn said could decide her to drive into town with them. It was Canaria's "Oh, please," that melted her resolve, her face a lost little island.

MANHATTAN'S sequined streets twinkled fresh as a morning sea through Canaria's eyes. They went shopping together, heard the Philharmonic in an all-Beethoven program, saw the Paul Klee exhibit at the Modern Museum, went everywhere she usually walked alone. Lunching at Top of the Sixes, they looked out at the steep windows to the streets where they had shopped, mazing far below them.

In their laughing delight, a hostess took them for mother and daughter.

"No, of course not —" iced through and out of her at being taken for a P.R. But of course — the hostess had mistaken Canaria for an American *cultured enough* to be her daughter.

As if they were in a spotlight, on a stage with all the world watching, Canaria reached a gold-wrapped gift across the high-placed table — a pin of Spanish silver chased to a sailing ship. Lynn watched beaming as she pinned it on. She couldn't help flushing at being mistaken for the girl's mother. She wore her shame as she wore the pin; she fumbled it and had to allow Canaria to come around to her and secure the safety clasp.

That night she took the train back to Westhampton Beach, saying she would be back at the Waldorf for the wedding. The day before the day before the wedding passed, and then the day before. She did not sleep that night, and in the night chill, the town took autumn on its back, full red and yellow. The house smelled of her husband's law books and legal papers, crate on crate of their mementos. Hilda had prepared a snack and started up a fire in the fireplace, but still the books and papers smelled of leaf mold.

Even with the morning, the leaf-burning streets shouted autumn after her. Her dressing room was decked with all the proper attire for the wedding, which Hilda laid out with a trust so implicit between them that she hadn't even looked in on the arrangements. There would be, as always, the right clothes for the right occasion, and a small trunk in case she decided to stay on at the Waldorf for a day or two, for her daughter's arrival.

Since it was early, she dressed hurriedly for the beach, for the blue and gold summer of the dunes. The ocean was still warm with summer, warmer than early July, and she walked, walked fast up shore, fast and far, walked until it was too late to dress, too late for the car to come for her, too late for the wedding.

KITE AWAY

IT ONLY TOOK two words: "Kites — let's."
"You mean, go fly a kite?"
"No, come — come fly a kite with me."
"Where? With television wires, tall buildings, traffic —"
"We'll find where."
From a window of kites, Marilyn ran into the store, asking for the kite aisle; selected a yellow bird for Dave, a bluebird for herself.
"This is damfolery."
"Damfoolery. Here, take the yellow. My treat."
"The question is still, where?"
"Central Park?"
"Too much downdraft — too many trees."
Dave fingertipped her thread-straight hair that glistered like Venetian glass, the round hazel eyes gold-green entangled.
"We could take the tubes to Jersey City, Marilyn. Near where I had my first accounting job, there is a broken-down park with a huge ballfield, swampy somewhat around the edges."
Down in the Path train tubes, Marilyn held the kites preciously, hurried the escalator up to May winds. With the children in school, ball players at work, the field was theirs. They breathed in the magnolias, damp grasses, stagnant waters of the pond. Easy kites to assemble. Cross-sticks fitted neatly into two plastic slots. No tail.
Two hundred and fifty feet of kite string on a cardboard cylinder. They ran with their kite birds, trying on the winds — North, East — no, West — beginning to lift, sighing back. South West did it — lifted Marilyn's kite highest. She willed it into flight, blue eyes to blue kite to blue sky — all three May shining.
Dave sank to the grass with an immediate cord problem, his clump so swampy, he moved muttering and wiping, to a dryer tuft.
"Had enough?" he called. But Marilyn was way across the field, her hair rippling like a kite-tail.
While he sat with his downed kite, no longer trying to untangle the string, her blue wing danced the cloudless. He went into his backpack, opened his Times to the financial page.
Marilyn's kite tugged so hard to be free, it wrenched the string from her hand. She flew after it with her eyes, across the ballfield to a stand of pines where it seemed to drop.

"That's that," said Dave. "There is still time to —"

"Time to go after my kite."

"Don't be ridiculous. That kite is probably across the thruway by now, if it isn't ripped by the pine branches. All this over a stupid dollar-fifty kite. I'll buy you a better one."

"I want *that* kite. I'll go where it leads."

"Marilyn — Marilyn — listen" he called after her. "If you're not back in ten minutes, I'll leave without you."

"But I don't know the way back. We turned down so many streets."

"Ten minutes. I mean it." He drew out his chin to the limits.

Narrowing her blues against the sun, Marilyn scanned the pines. No kite caught in the piercing needles. She asked the workers laying cement, the park attendant spearing papers, even peered into trash cans.

Black with traffic, the thruway had no stop lights. Many scary starts before blind running to banshee brakes.

A chain fence so high she needed a boost from a couple of hokey players, and an ease down from the ballplayers.

The ten minutes were up. No Lot's wife, she didn't look back to where Dave might or might not be; climbed a hill of cherry blossoms in deepest pink. To where — where was she going? Easier to reach the horizon than an unseeable kite. She would like to drop down to the petaled earth, and rest. Fall asleep most like — she couldn't risk. Not once had she looked up. Triumph of cherry confetti at seeing her bluebird flying high. Felt her cheeks reddening over the thought of her kite string in a thief's grubby hand.

Hair pink-petaled, flying with the kite wind, she ran down the hill to a field at the Spring start of wild flowers.

Thief caught with the kite string in his hand. Marilyn's fingers tingled for the tug of having while setting free.

Dark hair on the bristle side went with a chin he could never tuck as Dave did in though. Honest denims without glitter and fancy patches.

"Sir — Sir —" cut off her breathless. "That's my kite."

"Your kite — *your* kite? It belongs to the winds."

"Come on — cut the semantics — it's mine — my kite. Suppose you give it back to me."

"Suppose I don't. A kite is where the joy is."

His the joy, all right — denim blue his eyes looking up into the blue. Hers more violet-blue — both for looking out to sea or up to the kite-flying skies.

"Here, let's fly the kite together." He gave her a twist of cord.

Had to lean towards him, the better to fly the kite. His breath reminded her of reading how Walt Whitman had a breath like field flowers. Field flowers as they danced the kite higher — higher.

They were one person flying a kite, feeling the upper winds.

Dave — Dave back there — where back there?

PROSE
POEMS

BAMBOO AT THE GRAVE

BOWED HEADS, Aunt Ellen's, Aunt Laura's, her sister's — bowed but askancing her yellow dress — yes, yellow, golden yellow, hue of sun and life, Dad's favorite, to see him off on this, his greatest journey ... " 'that if our earthly house dissolved, we have a building of God'..." The new minister's voice washed over the death fact of the casket in its smother of flowers ... " 'an house not made with the hands, eternal in the heavens' "... His head high, hair yellow-gold, maize, drawing what light the winter elms let through to the living room-head high, but inclined, listening, as if he had an inside wire to God.

Away at school she'd heard about the new minister; how people stood at the doors to hear him preach; how he brought the church to new life, sometimes mistaking the pulpit for a soap box, crowding the community auditorium; how everyone turned to look after the young minister when he walked head high and hatless along the street. Married, wouldn't you know, Edith had written, with three small towheads.

"A scientist," he was saying, "whose chemical discoveries brought him the Willard Gibbs medal, yet his scientific knowledge only deepened his belief in the unknowable ..."

Walks with him a runway to the universe, talking of xylem under the stars, crossing fields to study geological beginnings, bending over glacial striae, climbing a mountainside that had been folded and faulted in ancient upheaval, discovering the universe in the galaxies or the veining of a flower. No, don't burn tears over those walks; now he can walk with you always.

Emma's glance spaded for the next to die — their brother Dave in a service uniform that needed growing into, Uncle George holding onto his two canes, Aunt Ellen with the cancerous spot widening on her cheek, or somebody quite unexpected. No time-tables for these journeys.

Emma early put away her dolls to pick at death with the grownups, their words a mess of eels around her own play .... *Exhumed the body, dug it up out of the grave ... her head kicked in by a horse, but the coffin was open ... can't wait too long or the jaw falls away to a grin ...* "Don't touch her, don't touch her; you'll get sick," some woman had screamed when she reached out to Nana, cheek cold as night.

" 'Thou hast the words of eternal life' " ... Emma rimmed him red with her eyes for a voice that laid a feast where flowers should be withering. Procession of caskets before the silvery pier glass that they always glanced into before starting out . . . the baby in such a little box, Les burned so badly that the lid was sealed, Mama an invalid on a day bed after Les, her wrists wasting beneath petaled cuffs.

The big old house must be more livable for Dad, she'd decided at Mama's grave. Her courses in interior decoration must show her how. "Too frantically gay," her teacher had said of her designs. "Rooms too model." Dad would never work in the study she'd planned for him, never see the first sketches ... sobs beating around inside like those birds that used to get trapped in the attic. Emma, ready to stiffen her nostrils at anything audible, took satisfied count of tears, duly silent, from a sister who wouldn't view the body, or sigh over the embalmer's art ... so lifelike ... a smile on his lips ... no pain.

Dad couldn't stand between her and Emma this time .... "Leave Hesper alone. She doesn't have to look just because it happens to be the custom. She wants only the living image" Not bloodless in a coffin, the paralyzed cheek, the twisted hand. Dad has no time to be back here with a cast-off body; he is with her, his living self, even as he goes on to prepare a place for her.

Youngsters slamming down their sleds outside, runners scraping at the melted edges of the hill. " 'For the things which are seen are temporal' " ...His head the only radiance in a room of shadows, yet he could look deaths-head, skin stretched tight over high cheek-bones, the nostrils bared like skull holes.

Death images in a worm crawl through these burial customs. Dad would get a kick out of talking over his own funeral; he'd recall ancient mores — the mourner's shadow that must not cross the grave lest his soul be buried with the dead; the Karens who stretched bamboo sticks into the open grave and called to their souls to climb back out of it to their bodies.

The voice had stopped circling; sounds of the big old house were closing in, dripping eaves in a February thaw, melting snow down the drain-pipe, coal settling in the bin as if Dad had just thrown a shovelful on the furnace and was coming back upstairs.

Stir and creak of chairs toward the grave, a further obeisance to body rot. Emma was outdoing the funeral director in preparations for the parade of the remains through the streets. Maybe all this busyness was Emma's way of staying with life. The death and the dying had been Emma's while she was away at school. Dave in his ill-fitting uniform shouldn't be here at all staring into the deaths-head.

Coming out to the porch, she felt a death chill from all the other times ... the pillar bruised by the hammock rope, wet earth at the frayed edges of snow, voracious earth, the decayed smell of it ... sun up there beyond the eaves, so pale you could stare into it as a moon in shrouds and vapors, a ball on a gravestone.

Emma sat beside her, withered into Mama's sealskin, inheritor of funerals. Up the long hill to Elmwood, skid chains clanked the dirge; cars held back from the bad luck of breaking a funeral procession; faces chilled at their passing, their advertisement for life as ending in the grave.

Elmwood bleak as Emma's bones — skeletal trees, the doleful drip from snow-streaked monuments and mausoleums, wet little lambs and angels, snow lying heavy on some graves, falling away from others to the remains of autumn, earth frozen and earth in ooze.

They walked toward the canopy in the bone-eating damp ... Mama's funeral in May with the chestnuts and locusts in bloom, the jonquils she had planted for Mama to see from her window.

No one could clamp iron rings in her eyes and force her to look at the turned earth, the open grave, the monument with the old names worn thin, the new cut deep, and room for names to come, names, dates — *From-To* — when it should be the birth date to life eternal.

Branches with dead leaves still chattering, tree trunks creaking like coffin ropes, rose granite in the jonquil light across the hill. Stand back, don't let your shadow slip into the open grave. Grass in the melt, a mess of worms writhing back underfoot. Their whitish breath at the grave's edge, miasma of death, as they bowed before the earth, taker of all, the body embalmed, coffin copper-sealed, to delay the taking.

<171>

The new minister's hair bright-winged the sun struggling with its vapors. Say beyond the death service at graveside, say something sky-opening, light and life.

Dead leaves, dead whisperings, branches creaking in the wind, and his rote words like a trickle of earth to the grave.

Over now — all power given to death. Emma would go back to tidy up her grief, her sense of direction placing him in the earth of Elmwood beside Mama and the others, when the snows deepen, when the rain washes down the hill and the first leaves try their green. Dave would see body death in Korea, the kind no burial artist can prettify. Could be Dave — Emma in a fever over getting the body back in its closed box, having it dug up if necessary, brought here to rot in this particular earth ... No, don't think ....

The lift to the new minister's head, the listening — ask him, are they right, these burial customs that turn the dark into cold-sweating terror, that bell body death across the infinite? If he could know what they do to the child ... "Could you, do you think"— her voice back along the bamboo stick, bloodless but back — "could you possibly come home with us? I need very much to talk to you."

His eyes burned through the deaths-head. He helped her down a slope that was beginning to ice over, her skirt glimpsing yellow like the first flowers from brushed-back snow.

[*Prairie Schooner*, Winter 1953]

FROM THIS WINDOW

Two lights are burning on the pier — two altar lights without an altar.

Men are cutting a window in a wall.

Gold whorls, crystal whorls, iron rails, steps, scrolls, sills, bricks, flutterings — are the buildings here in the windows there.

Something trembles in the pane-dark sky — something trembles on the masts of ships.

Legs are white on whiter beds.

White on the sign-post branches of Columbia Heights are PIERPONT — WILLOW.

Men are cutting a window in a wall.

White light hews sockets in the face that fronts the page.

A sea gull lifts a little spray to claret.

Evergreens are rooted in a window-box of stone.

Beside a bed, the man winds his watch.

Window scratches bleed.

At the dead end of this street are two tree shadows — one tree.

Against the New York harbor, a house is heavy with sandstone slabs.

VEEDOL MOTOR OILS VEEDOL MOTOR OILS VEEDOL MOTOR OILS letter a ship red. Spray lifts to — VEEDOL MOTOR OILS. Smoke colors to — VEEDOL MOTOR OILS. Gulls dip to — VEEDOL MOTOR OILS VEEDOL MOTOR OILS VEEDOL MOTOR OILS.

All the ones across the way are shadows in their light.

Ships and piers and buildings are a mist about to clear.

A plot of ground is a hyphen between the sandstone slabs of the heavy house and the sandstone slabs of the boarded house.

Facets of a fountain, facets of a jewel, facets of a rocket are the lights on the ferry.

Leaves tire of their green.

Skirts harbor-rose, braids harbor-gold, steps harbor-gold-quick, a little girl dances.

Barges cross with trains.

Two censors — the boarded house and the heavy house — read the ships before passing them.

Something trembles in the pane-dark sky.

Curtains part — a head looks out — a terrier's head.

This cone of lime-colored light enters the pane across the way — goes into the room — goes deeper than the room — is a light in space — a light flung back.

Bronze on sandstone, at the dead end of Willow Street, spells COLUMBIA HEIGHTS SEMINARY.

Across the harbor, an electric sign flashes on, flashes off, flashes on, flashes off, flashes on, flashes off.

In all the dark windows there is a golden count of passing cars.

A sign lettered VACANCY sways.

Moon pale curtains almost open to rooms beyond rooms — halls beyond halls.

Shriveled leaves from the shadow tree are sparrows pecking for food at the roots of the wizened hedge.

Window scratches bleed.

Shale blue light from the clouded sun, settles on the farther shore, on the malachite towers of Ellis Island, the boats, the factories, the wind-patterned bay.

A hyphen of earth separates the Columbia Heights Seminary from the clay brown house where a matron in grey polices the floors.

The placard of the clay house reads OSBORNE PROBATION-ARY HOME FOR YOUNG WOMEN.

The rust-red house with the plump stone flowers, flirts its curtains.

Beyond this street, a wrinkled tower poises a ball about to topple.

Trunk to tail, great ships leave the harbor ring.

She gripes in her flesh with a soiled corset.

Sea horses arch their necks in sky water.

On the roof of the rust-red house is a black cloaked room whose window confronts space.

Past the censor, edges a dark prow, a great-a small prow.

Above the wheat gold dancing floor in the house of clay, stockings are drawn to legs, brassieres to breasts, girdles to thighs.

Tossing aside the curtains, a child stands naked. Hands snatch her.

Whirling ventilator spheres above galleried windows, hack with their scythes, the star caught among them.

Needles of the sun stitch wind-frayed water.

A few leaves tremble on the tree of this street. They are sparrows. They fly away.

Children skip past the COLUMBIA HEIGHTS SEMINARY.

Barges heaped with sand-gold lumber, barges heaped with coal, barges heaped with crushed stone sparkles, trample wavelets, flower blue.

Jewel points flash on the motor car beside the heavy house.

Red lights mark a one way street — the port side of ships — old stars.

He winds his watch.

Smoke distills sun-flame to rose.

Clouds are tawny leaves translated to light.

The harbor is a blue-flowered spread too often laundered.

Beneath dahlia curtains in the house of clay, a wheat gold dancing floor reaps dancing feet.

Something flashes — something on a lifting bar of grey. The bar is an arm — the flash a watch upon it. They are lifted to a chest convulsed with coughing.

As the gull takes wing, its image is limned in light upon the water.

This room projected by this window has a star upon its cornice — no ending to its walls.

Evergreens are rooted in a window-box of stone.

On a bed in the house of clay, she lies with legs drawn up — glances —parts them — glances.

From beneath a wind-racked shade, light starts out — a nerve exposed.

Frayed school curtains fluttering on the window ledge are an old maid's fingers on piano keys.

Light sets afloat the stranded shore.

Barges cross with trains.

Sun prints on sandstone are the seals of the maker, telling age.

Pigeon's offal frescoes the boarded house.

Mist is the exhalation of millions.

In chemise they posture at a window above the wheat gold dancing floor. The matron arms them back — jerks down the shade.

Arteries of a vine bulge on the rough side-wall of the house whose sandstone front sparkles.

Cadaver white is the drawn shade of the heavy house.

Up it gleams — up with the dredge — a fragmenting, crystal city — earth.

Something darts among jade and walnut — something horn-blende sleek and rapier long. It is a cane. A hand wields it — the hand of a man in a wheel chair.

Gulls are stones scudded by little boys.

Curtains part — a head looks out — a terrier's head.

Facets of a fountain, facets of a jewel, facets of a rocket are the lights on the ferry.

Rain chalk-marks the school.

In all the dark windows there is a golden count of passing cars. Sockets front the page.

The farther shore is the rose gold dusk of the shawl about the woman sewing at a window of the heavy house.

A dark prow, a great — a small prow.

Curls touch organdy as she bends over her sewing in the house of clay. Lifting her head, she waves and signals. The matron comes. Curls touch organdy.

Every window is closed — every curtain placed. The sky is polished clean. The harbor is swept of boats.

Cloud shriveled moon leaf trembles above harbor dark.

Coming into a furnished room, she hides her head in the furnished pillow.

The light on the pier tells how black the water.

A sign lettered VACANCY sways.

The man in the wheel chair lifts his cane to a baton, a golf club, a billiard cue, a gun.

Behind school curtains, a rising shadow tries to shake off the room.

Dolphins of light skim the bay.

Beneath the headboard of the bed, there is a long mound.

Vine comes to new leaf — snow leaf.

Cat's eye swift, the yellow green iris of the harbor closes about its pupil.

One comes down the street and in every ash can finds something — another comes down the street and in every ash can finds something — another comes down the street and in every ash can finds something.

Moon pale curtains almost open to rooms beyond rooms — halls beyond halls.

Ice golden is the sun — a glacier melting to streams which deposit rosy stones in the blue dark valleys of the sky.

Barges cross with trains.

The chauffeur helps a little woman down the steps of the heavy house.

A swarm of gnats caught by four red stacks is the farther shore.

A window confronts space.

Coming into a furnished room, she nails her pictures to the walls.

Window scratches bleed.

A gold star on a copy book, one light shines in the school.

Mist is the exhalation of millions.

Spreading sail, a dark cloud skims the harbor. It washes to peach to jonquil, to white. Snowflakes try the air.

The sun is a blood-red crystal in the garden of clouds.

Star blue is the searchlight on the bay.

Evergreens have snow behind them — hills and hills of it, back and back and — snow is lamplight on the pane.

Gulls are crests — crests are gulls — gulls are fragments of ice in the tide — fragments of ice are gulls.

White velvet slips from the shoulders of a titian-haired girl in the house of sand sparkles. She draws it up — lets it slip —glances.

Beyond wayward snow, the harbor pales to the blue of eyes in tears.

A dark prow, a small — a great prow.

The electric sign flashes on, flashes off, flashes on, flashes off, flashes on, flashes off.

This room has a star upon its cornice — no ending to its walls.

Harbor gold quick the little girl dances.

Snow railings, snow balconies, signposts, chimney pots, ventilators rising to dark clouds are Indian pipes on a forested hill.

Curtains part — a head looks out — a terrier's head.

Birches are the spars and cables — a crocus the glow on the mast.

Her flesh churns as thickly she butters a slab of bread.

Pigeons are blue white — ice is blue white. The feet of pigeons are rosy-water is rosy.

All the ones across the way are shadows in their light.

Bones are the spars and cables — phosphorescence, the glow on the mast.

Kneeling before a sun-gold mirror, she squeezes blackheads.

Bats in blue light, charred fragments ride from the chimney — dip low, fly high-disturbing a star.

On a bed in the house of clay, dark hair spreads wings between restless thighs.

Behind the evergreens and their snow hills, four hold cards.

Trunk to tail, great ships leave the harbor ring.

The lamp on her hair is fire — moon on the skylight, ice.

Ships and shores and buildings are a mist about to clear.

Beyond a holly wreath in the house of clay, curling irons flash to hair, lipsticks to lips, perfume phials to ear lobes, to breasts.

Shears upthrust, one girl rushes at another — gores her flesh.

Snow white vapor in ice blue sky refracts to the iridescence of humming birds' wings.

Dark hair trembles on the pillow as men carry the stretcher to the ambulance.

On the drawn shade of the heavy house rests the shadow of a Christmas wreath.

Brands in the charred sky, smoulder.

Lighted smoke is a new world forming.

A man coming into a furnished room, pours himself a drink —
goes out.

A dark prow, a great — a small prow.

In bony grasp, school curtains tremble.

A skater parting pine branches, the girl flings wide the curtains.

Light shines from the cane held rigid.

Sockets front the page.

Two make love — they separate — they are both men.

Four hold cards.

Dandruff on shoulders is snow on the conical tower.

White smoke whiter than the mist — white surf whiter than the
smoke — white gulls whiter than the surf are less white than the
wreath of funeral roses on the house whose front sparkles.

Six men in one road shovel a dole of snow — lift it slowly to the
truck; inch their shovels back along a pavement almost picked bare
of snow; dig for scraps.

Light of the window against space, before it becomes fully itself,
goes to nothing.

The sky fractures to white radiance — radiance crumples to dust
— dust is snow blown from a wire.

He winds his watch.

Blue ice on copper-smooth water, the green of the sky when the sun swings low, blue ice where the windows of ships drop sunset fire, cuts the flesh of the bay-drawing blood.

Moon pale curtains almost open to rooms beyond rooms — halls beyond halls.

Thirteen windows of the school are frosted.

Hair of titian eddies to snow as the girl reaches for the box on the window ledge.

This cone of lime-colored light enters the pane across the way— goes into the room — goes deeper than the room — is a light in space — a light flung back.

Snow the grey of fertilizer takes ashes the gold of seed.

Ships in ice are plants without chlorophyll.

A sign lettered VACANCY sways.

The clouded moon is a pane the wind tires of polishing.

Facets of a fountain, facets of a jewel, facets of a rocket are the lights of the ferry.

Millions of windows twinkle in the walls of night.

A girl sits staring. On the other side of the wall a boy sits staring.

Beneath dahlia curtains, the wheat gold dancing floor reaps dancing feet.

Moon brings the skylight from blackness to the grey of a dying mouth — from grey to moon flesh, moon sky, moon sand — to ash blond hair brushed smooth — porcelain, quartzite, arrested lightning — a rift in the night.

Moon returns the skylight to arrested lightning, quartzite, porcelain, smooth hair, moon sand, moon sky, moon flesh, a dying mouth —black.

Curtains part — a head looks out — a terrier's head.

Towers of the island are golden planes taking flight.

This window room has a star upon its cornice — no ending to its walls.

Ships white with ice on a dark bay are May-flies dead upon a screen.

Flags with blood-red stripes and white stars on heaven blue, mark the houses of this street.

Glancing, leaning back, glancing, she parts her legs. Light thrusts deep the pane.

Moon rays on harbor ice are ships arriving as they start — starting as they arrive.

Smoke distills sun flame to rose.

Kittens holding up their tails and slyly stepping, are tugs in an alley of black ripples.

The harbor in ice is a field white with bloom!

Gold chalk on a blackboard, one light shines in the school.

Harbor magma seethes to crystals of quartz and feldspar; to horneblende, olivine, topaz. Boats are basalt and gabbro in the midst of frothed glass.

Underclothing in a room is fungi in a hollow.

Willow gold shade, red winged chair, silt black table are tattoed in mist.

Barges cross with trains.

Squirrels whisking brush from a cache, fingers in the house of clay whisk back curtains.

In all the dark windows, there is a golden count of passing cars.

The gullied tower is a hill in rain.

Sockets front the page.

Stars are drops of water percolating through a cavern roof.

Within a cocoon of mist, something stirs — something dark and long.

A yellow bird from a thicket, light springs up.

Rain on the harbor is white of uncurling ferns — rain beside the heavy house is the violet grey of a black flecked mirror.

Vans stop before the school.

The little girl with roller skates and a dove blue coat; the little boy with bicycle and aviator's suit are playing with the colored boy whose sweater is faded, his shirt white and smoothly ironed. A woman motions at the window. Another woman motions at the window.

The colored boy sits alone on the basement steps, and spits and spits.

Men are glassing in the great roof.

A chauffeur helps the little woman into her car.

The great roof is a false ship with masts and stacks and wavelets of light.

Clouds spell. Across sky slate washed clean, an aeroplane rising crystal, dipping black, pencils cloud letters J-E-L-L-O. Wind distended, they rupture.

The harbor is a dark star passing through nebula.

He winds his watch.

White green spray at rosy prows reaches toward rosy wings in green atmosphere.

Branches on the tree of this street rough to rose pointed green.

From the windows curtains are being taken; on the porches rugs are being beaten; into cellars coal is being poured.

Sun rays in the room of jade and walnut are the strings of a tennis racket.

Mist on the bay is breath upon window glass.

A dark prow, a great-a small prow.

Dahlia curtains are being gathered, soot pollen shaking from them. The dancing floor is a fallow patch. Chairs huddle about a weathered piano.

Tiny wings are about to take off from branches. They are the beginning of leaves.

Boxes and barrels follow boxes and barrels follow boxes and barrels through the doorway of the school.

Trunk to tail, great ships leave the harbor ring.

Boxes and barrels follow boxes and barrels follow boxes and barrels.

Lights of the false ship ward off mist.

Shuddering throughout its length, a bookcase meets the dark of the van.

Patina on copper is grass on earth.

Harbor gold quick, the little girl dances.

A room high mirror reflects the van. A room high mirror reflects The Heights Seminary. An oval mirror reflects space.

Windows are polished brook clear.

A piano stool, spinning in earth rough hands, scatters dust, pollen gold.

Smoke is the milky way of rain.

One light — fourteen windows.

A cloud of white spores drift to the van from blackboard grey with erasures.

The evergreens of the window box are sere.

Smoke distills sun flame to rose.

Children watch school desks flounder into the van.

Stars are planes — planes are stars.

Bedposts, a gas heater, a ringed table, a dented trunk pass beneath the eyes of the grey-haired school mistress.

Shore lights are flowers springing back in the wake of a great ship.

The rocking chair rocks in the van.

Something trembles in the pane dark sky.

Something trembles on the masts of ships.

A gardener prepares the ground between the heavy house and the boarded house for plants already grown.

Flashes on, flashes off, flashes on, flashes off, flashes on, flashes off.

Ivy that scabs the side wall, filigrees the sparkling front.

Rose smoke is a flowering bush.

The workman's spathe pries the bronze letters C-O-L-U-M-B-I-A H-E-I-G-H-T-S S-E-M-I-N-A-R-Y from sandstone.

In all the dark windows there is a golden count of passing cars.

Ships and piers and buildings are a mist about to clear.

For every letter uprooted there is another bitten in stone.

He winds his watch.

Sea life in a sunken ship, wreckers swarm the school.

Hair is golden through the rain.

Stairs are broken off in space.

Shadows of floor boards divide walls into moon panels.

All the doors of the school are stacked.

This window room has a star upon its cornice — no ending to its walls.

An altar candle quivering within an altar cup, a gold dress stirs within white curtains.

The school mistress returns to where the school was. Her room is space.

Harbor forms are retained in ash of rose, rose blue, blue violet.

Moon pale curtains almost open to rooms beyond rooms — halls beyond halls.

Iron teeth bite into the earth where the seminary was. The harbor is shivered glass.

In the window lake, sere trees are green.

Through silt-dark mist, a man urges along a cart heaped with strawberries.

Sun in the heavy house is lace on a loom.

The scissors grinder unstraps his pack — stands staring at all the closed doors.

Sockets front the page.

Wind teases the lilacs in the vendor's cart.

Facets of a fountain, facets of a jewel, facets of a rocket are the lights on the ferry.

New walls stake their claim in space.

The lame boy and the colored one play together. Waves are the sun's toboggan slides.

Barges cross with trains.

A ragged woman wheels a baby carriage jouncing with violets.

Moon pale curtains are down. Paper-hangers work beneath electric bulbs in one small room with a hallway and a closet door.

The organ-grinder lifts his face to a wall of windows where heads recant.

A necklace of lights on the false ship heaves at the throat of the wind.

Curtains of the heavy house are stone behind glass.

A sign lettered VACANCY sways.

New window frames are stacked against the beginning of walls.

All the ones across the way are shadows in their light. Moon leeches suck the bay.

Flakes are whirling, rising, falling — down to wind valleys, up to wind hills. Flakes are brown, green — they are seeds. They drop from precipices of the wind — strike cement, strike macadam, strike iron, strike steel.

Set apart from harbor lights, stars are old favorites watching the new.

Light that shatters on coal, flowers on leaves.

Untwining her legs, a girl on the stone railing of the clay house returns the backward glance of a man. The matron taps her on the knee.

Shovelful by shovelful, sand slows the whitely boiling lime.

In the plot between the heavy house and the boarded house, the gardener turns the sprinkler on twelve tulips, four irises, and one bush.

A silver tray, moon silver, shines beyond a shade of green — deep forest green.

Curtains, the brown of suntanned arms, gather in the air.

A dark prow, a great — a small prow.

Flags with blood red stripes and stars on heaven blue mark the houses of this street.

Aeroplanes are sunspots above water fire. A battleship is the smoke of water fire — another battleship is smoke of water fire — another battleship is smoke — another, another and another — smoke.

Her legs are uneasy on the bed — her hair crushes into the open book on the pillow.

Rain beneath the street lamp hammers out a flower image on the macadam above the earth.

Moon on the bay is the distillation of a million light years.

Flesh tone is folded in roses — rose tone is folded in flesh.

Staggering beneath the street lamp, he unbuttons his trousers. A pale stream shivers to the pavement.

Straw packing around a gift is sun in the room of jade and walnut.

Clouds before the wind, battleships leave the harbor.

Up goes her skirt as reeling in the shadow of the clay house, she starts to wriggle out of her clothes. The boy with her runs away. The matron opens the door.

Lights on water red with sun are beads of lymph on infected flesh.

Two stand talking — between them the one man's greyhound, the other man's broom.

Ships and piers and buildings are a mist about to clear.

He winds his watch.

Over the golden thigh of the harbor, smoke draws black lace chemise.

Gulls are white flames against a purple sky.

Ivy is electric.

This cone of lime colored light enters the pane across the way, — goes into the room — goes deeper than the room.

Ships' windows are decanters of ruby glass on blue and platinum brocade.

Curtains part — a head looks out — a terrier's head.

Shutters close over windows of the heavy house. Steps are boarded.

Up in the fountain's crystal fingers — up on the lawn of the heavy house, millions of sun balls are being juggled. Sun balls drop to the bodies of children a-tumble in the new cut grass.

This window has a star upon its cornice — no ending to its walls.

Fuchsia tipped cigarettes bud on branches of the dark.

Bathed in white, the dredge withdraws from the harbor.

Stripped to the waist, their backs clay brown, workmen sweat to build walls, sweat to build ceilings, sweat to build windows in the walls.

Lights looped across the bay are lights on a roller coaster, and the boats are the little boats of the love ride.

Flags with blood red stripes mark the houses of this street.

Foam at the prow of the sky, bursting rockets fall beneath starred masts.

The gardener, a woman and a little girl are vine close to the heavy house. All the shuttered windows rise above them.

In and out of smoke, harbor lights are fireflies among bushes.

Something trembles in the pane dark sky.

Sockets front the page.

Stars are phosphorescent life in the lower ocean of space.

The quick-opening door of the clay house jerks shadow weeds from the porch where boys and girls entwine.

Curtains fluttering against pale yellow walls are pink moths upon the night-blooming primrose.

Pink clouds hover above the lights of the false ship.

In all the dark windows there is a golden count of passing cars.

Flashes on, flashes off, flashes on, flashes off, flashes on, flashes off.

Trunk to tail, great ships leave the harbor ring.

Path of a lighted ship comes to path of the moon. Light loses to light.

Mist is the exhalation of millions.

Chairs are set upon sun-petaled porches. Hands sink to laps, droop from chair arms, lie with carven stillness on railings of stone.

A dark — a great prow.

Workmen walk steel.

A sign lettered VACANCY sways.

Facets of a fountain, facets of a jewel, facets of a rocket are the lights on a ferry.

Smoke distills sun flame to rose.

Lightning splits the harbor geode.

Barges cross with trains.

Harbor gold quick, the little girl dances.

A window confronts space.

Boats are insects hovering near the corolla of the sun.

A whip of light from the quick-opening door of the clay house ensnares the two in each other's arms.

The harbor is a blackboard grey with erasures.

All the ones across the way are shadows in their light.

The sun is an outgrowth of the rose mycelium that webs the water and eats into the wood of the pier.

A spade of lightning strikes harbor metal.

Ships and piers and buildings are a mist about to clear.

He winds his watch.

Children play in the sand pile beside new walls.

Smoke-blue atmosphere enfolds hands that lie still on stone.

A dark prow — a small prow.

Sun lava flows down the cloud mountains — drops to the conical
tower.

Curtains part — a head looks out.

[From "A Little Anthology of The Poem in Prose,"
edited by Charles Henri Ford,
in *New Directions in Prose & Poetry.* No 14, 1953]

ABOUT THIS BOOK

The body type for this book is Aldine, designed by Hermann Zapf to complement his earlier typeface Palatino. Aldine is named after Aldus Manutius, the great Renaissance humanist printer and publisher, who based his font designs on letterforms from Roman stone carvings. Titles are set in variants of Franklin Gothic, one of the great classic display faces of the early 20th Century. When this face was designed by Morris Fuller Benton in 1902, the term "Gothic" was used to describe modern-looking sans-serif typefaces, quite contrary to today's conception of "Gothic." Although the face has had many competitors, and faded from view between the two World Wars, its use resurged in the 1940s. Its distinctive letterforms and legibility kept it in type catalogs through the phototypesetting era and well into the digital era. Since it was a "hot metal" font originally, it also blends well with the urban cityscape engravings chosen for the cover. American wood engraver John DePol (1913-2004) consented to have details from four of his engravings used as covers for this series. DePol grew up in Greenwich Village and drew locales around Emilie Glen's Barrow Street residence since his childhood.